PATRICIA Q. BIDAR

PARDON ME FOR MOONWALKING

THE CONTENTS

PARDON ME
FOR
MOONWALKING

COMPANY

There's a tap at the door—too soft to be called a knock. The Equity and Inclusion meeting is ending, so I jab the LEAVE button as I smile and wave: Goodbye!

My legs have stiffened in the sitting position. It's still early, but already getting purple out there. The tall hedge my father planted outside the front window years ago renders winter-dark my at-home work corner.

I crack the front door to reveal an old man with a drooping mustache. Beside him is a pony, brown and white. A horseshoe of synthetic red roses hangs from the pony's neck. On a strap around the man's own neck hangs a camera. His eyes are lugubrious.

"Are you serious?" I say.

"Old fashioned, I know," he says. "We live not far from here. Around from the liquor store. Are there any . . . children in the home?" It turns out he's making a little money taking Polaroid photos of neighborhood kids atop his tiny horse. I am old enough to remember such photographers, such businesses. Very long ago.

"No kids. But I grew up in this neighborhood," I say.

The block has changed. There used to be a lot of pride here. Now it's all burnt lawns, cracked stucco, and steel security doors. The palm trees seem drained of their life force. "This was my parents' place," I say. I don't add, *And now I'm back.*

"Madam, I can see you're otherwise engaged . . ." His sad eyes take in my eyeliner, my blouse and earrings, my sweats and bare feet. His jacket is thin. Door-to-door photos? Failure lives behind those eyes. He's not even making a pitch.

His little horse shifts and blinks. "She's thirsty, you see," he says at last. To demonstrate, the man lifts the horse's upper lip. He presses gently on her gum near the upper teeth. "The pink should return more quickly than this."

"You could have just asked for water," I say. I have never been this close to a horse. Their giant eyeballs have always unnerved me. "Hang on." In the kitchen, I fill a cereal bowl with tap water. When I return, the man and the horse are in my living room, standing in front of the Christmas tree. The little horse nuzzles fallen pine needles.

"She sure seems to enjoy that water," I say as we watch her drink. These two are the first living things in here all year, other than me and last summer's mosquitos. I discreetly inhale, trying to find the man's scent. English Leather?

"This old girl and me, we're best friends," he is saying. His voice is felty. "We take care of each other." Tears spring to my eyes and I squeeze them back in.

The horse finishes her water and I take them on a tour of the house. That's what people do now, isn't it? Give tours of their houses when people come over? I don't remember anyone doing that when I was growing up.

The man nods and murmurs appreciation for my spare rooms, one of which still houses my father's home bar with its unlit Hamm's and Olympia beer lights. I created a decoupage sign for him when I was twelve: magazine-ripped images of a naked flapper, a fanned-out royal flush, and a bottle of Hennessy. Above the pictures, I stenciled, "What's Your Pleasure?" The other guest room is just my mother's Hammond

Solovox organ, coated with a thin layer of dust I haven't noticed before.

"Well, I have a meeting," I say, and I hear in my voice the regret that our visit is ending so soon. The old man says cheerfully that they'll see themselves out. It really was good, the normalcy of having someone in here. I turn my office chair around so I'm riding it cowgirl style. That feels off, so I remove my underpants and sweats and try again. I must have the time wrong for the meeting because the camera returns only my own face, looking pallid. I sit there breathing in my square. I utilize a feature that adds coral lipstick to my mouth, and prettily shaped brows above my glasses. But I see now that when I move my head, the simulated lips and brows drift fractionally behind.

When I hit LEAVE, I worry I'll find a mound of horse droppings in the vestibule, or the front door yawning wide. Instead, the living room is neat as always. The only trace of them is a Polaroid photo of the man and the horse. The man is waving and smiling. I sniff the air hard for English Leather but detect no trace. The old-fashioned scent would have been company of a sort.

In the bathroom, I climb onto the sink, press my face close to the mirror. I manually lift my lip. I jab with my pointer finger the upper gum, watching the color recede and fill. White then pink then white then pink.

ORANGE, YELLOW, AND BLACK
OR
EVERYTHING IS ARCHIE

I

My kid brother Junior and I meet Archie and his pals in our cousins' pink-walled bedroom. Every Thanksgiving and Easter, we meet them again. Our cousins have a subscription. In the past, these cousins have told me and Junior jokes we do not understand. Now we have caught up, but our cousin-ly roles are already fixed.

Downstairs a regulation-size pool table awaits, covered in plywood and orange plastic tablecloths. Soon, the women and we kids will sit down to Thanksgiving dinner. The men will eat from TV trays in front of the game.

I am too old for Archie comics. I don't care. I feel the comic strip characters have wisdom to impart about my failed attempts at friendship. Yellow-haired Betty is like no one I have ever known: wholesome in gingham and shorts. She smells of vanilla and clean sweat. Black-haired Veronica, on the other hand, is like the Mean Carries at school. Nobody is rich in San Pedro, but strata exist and are never forgotten.

Veronica thinks love can be bought with money. The more you have, the better you are. She passes along her old clothes to Betty, who takes them politely but never wears them. Like the bags of clothes my mom insists on bringing here to our aunt's house, on these visits.

Sweet Betty is baking, her unmanicured toes in pink house shoes that bear no imprint of her feet. Meanwhile, Veronica's across town between the sheets at Archie's, insulting the meager thread count, Archie's no-name track shoes, the cry he emits when he cums. Like Betty, Archie is wary about taking what he is given.

II

Atop the springy cloud, Jughead sits too close. It's just another way he communicates. Since Jughead is almost always eating, he's a man of few words. Also, he is a leaner. Archie has long accepted that his old friend means nothing by this. Jughead's trademark porkpie hat has fallen a mile below them. His black hair is plastered to his head. Jughead is motivated by food, so Archie suspected his Groupon for cloud tasting would go over well with his old friend. He was right. The two finish their cloud samples, each lost in thought.

There is a television commercial for perfume. The claim is that the scent interacts with each and every woman, resulting in a completely unique scent. "Alls I'm saying is," Archie says, "Betty and Veronica probably taste different. *Down there.* Hand to God, I aim to find out."

"Betty?" Jugheads says at last. "Graham crackers. Tuna salad on toasted white." The besotted redhead catches a whiff of his friend's own musky scent. He shifts to hide his full body buzz.

"And Veronica?" Archie's voice cracks on the second syllable.

Jughead performs a chef kiss, then distracted, starts to lick his fingers.

The server brings the second tasting, more cirrus than cumulous. Purple, with lightning inside. This sample tastes of darker things. Archie thinks about the smell of his parents' bedroom on the weekends when his mother makes the bed carelessly or not at all. In his father's nightstand drawer is a small tub of Vaseline with a finger trough in the center. Sometimes after lunch, his orange-headed dad will say, "Come up and visit me, Momma," and his mother will duck her head and follow him up the stairs, leaving Archie to clear the table. On these afternoons, Martin Denny music seeps from under their door.

"Veronica?" Archie repeats, louder this time.

"Black cherry and fertilizer," Jughead answers, holding Archie's gaze with mock intensity until Archie cracks up, wishing he could trace Jughead's thin lips with his finger.

III

"Ants' brains are in their bottoms!" Betty says after she and Archie are settled in the blue velvet theater seats. It's the poor people theater: 99 cents for all shows before 3 PM. They are the only ones so far, but it's early. There is so much to appreciate about Betty. Her bare arms, with their faint spray of freckles; nothing like Archie's copper constellations. The way she leaves baked goods on his porch at night. She signals him by drumming her fingertips on his bedroom window before righting her bike and pumping home down the tree-lined street.

Archie agitates the popcorn tub in invitation and Betty shakes her head. She is dieting again. In any case, Betty is a cheap date, always suggesting this second run theater in the dying Riverdale mall, which the chain stores have all fled.

"Did you say ants?" he says to be polite. She probably has it wrong.

The theater is filling up fast. Mostly it is weary parents and their kids. Archie begins counting down backward by 100. When he reaches 49, the lights dim. Archie employs the same move he always does with the sweet blonde. Slides his palm into the opening of her checked blouse, gliding toward her pumping heart.

He does this because it is expected. In fact, Archie is hopelessly in love with his old friend Jughead. It is 1978. But like my brother Junior, Archie knows it is simply not safe to admit this.

An hour after our last high school final, Junior moves from San Pedro to San Francisco. He takes only a duffel bag, which he carries on his lap on the train. He wears a fedora hat. He is sixteen years old.

In San Pedro, Junior has been cornered and beaten up at least once. Another time, the Christian kids told me they wanted to talk to me about something very serious and then informed me they were concerned that my brother "might be attracted to males." They didn't want him to go to hell, they explained. I told them to move out of my fucking airspace.

Today Junior accepts their friend requests on social media with no hard feelings. I am not a big enough person to do this. I began marrying early and often. Moved a thousand miles away, then 3,000. Changed my name, my address, my hair color—orange, yellow, and black.

GONE BABY GONE

Arthur and I are lucky. A client of mine on 110th and Broadway—I clean houses—had a family thing and needed to leave the country for a few months. Arthur and I could stay.

It's late morning. The door buzzer sounds and Arthur springs up. His old friend, Joey Chestnut. What we know so far is that Joey's gotten clean, or at least a lot cleaner than the last time we saw him. He has a lady now. Maybe she's a calming influence. Now Arthur and Joey are going on a fishing weekend. They're traveling light because just yesterday Arthur's Pacer was towed.

Aw, Jesus.

Aw, Jeez.

This is their Staten Island greeting. Shoulders are smacked. I say hey. Joey's put on weight. This is good.

You want coffee? I say, and Joey says definitely.

Where's this woman you made up? Arthur asks, and Joey says she's downstairs with her friend.

From the kitchenette I can look down and see. Sure enough, there are two women on the sidewalk in front of the stoop on the basketball court side, smoking. They're both wearing fur-collared coats and platform shoes. Okay, so she's real.

If it weren't for my client needing to leave the country, I don't know where we'd be staying right now, because of all the mess Arthur caused at our old building. My client said we've got to keep our noses down, avoid the other neighbors, and above all do not call the super for any reason.

So far, it has gone great. My client's not a richie. Part of her disability payment provides house cleaning. I don't know where she gets the rest of her money. I mind my business. I have friends who get high with their clients. Eat with them. Not me.

—the best thing that ever happened to me, Joey is saying. *You* know where I was at after high school.

Arthur murmurs something supportive. And then Joey is saying he's really gotten his shit together and alls he brought for the whole weekend is chicken tranquilizers and a handle of Wild Turkey. It'll be like the old days.

Now Joey is laughing—he actually pronounces the words hee hee hee—about our heavy door and our various locks. I guess he thinks this is our apartment.

Oh, this place is a regular Fort Knox, Arthur says. Self-important with his thick mustache and mutton chops. The river and Columbia are easy walking distance, he adds. St. John's, too.

A real lord of the manor, I think but do not say.

Joey steps back into the hall, where he's left his bag and the fishing rods. The door closes behind him with its heavy click. I'm always worried about locking myself out. We only have one key.

So, what do you think? I ask Arthur, and he says he thinks it'll be okay.

What about those girls? They'd better not be coming with.

Nah, they're just with Joey. They're with Joey. Accompanied him here, is all. And I can hear now that the girls have come upstairs. Someone must've let them in. They're talking fast and their voices bounce against the enameled walls. I can't make anything out.

Arthur makes a big thing of taking my chin in his hand and tipping my face up to his for a kiss. He tries to hike my skirt up, but I'm wearing my quilted maxi and it's a lot of fabric. I say Arthur's gonna start pounding on the door and he says no he won't. Arthur takes my chin and tips my face for a kiss. And then he's hiking my skirt up. Oh, Arthur. The things he gets me to do. I step up onto the couch and sway strip-tease style, adding a dip to shuck my skirt and panties. Arthur throws them across the room. He's kissing my tits and kissing my tits and it just lights me up; my whole body buzzes with want.

I say, Joey's gonna start pounding and he says no he won't and we're kissing again. And I'm lying on the couch with my feet touching the floor when Arthur enters me with full urgency and oh. Oh. Then he's finished, our bare chests, our rib cages, pressed together. I taste the salt of his face. He pushes up, dips to kiss my neck saying thank you thank you thank you. I belong to this man. Oh, Arthur.

I wash the coffee cups and the pot, thinking about a job I have at three, a gay couple in the village. I switch on WNEW and it's Patti Smith, a girl singer from New Jersey. If Arthur were here, he'd say turn that shit off.

That's when I hear it: the next-door neighbor lady screaming: she's been robbed. I run out to the hall and she's there with her laundry from the basement machines, and she's telling me she propped the door with a matchbook and down in the laundry all of five minutes. And it hits me: those girls are thieves and I'm good and locked out barefoot in just my maxi skirt. Arthur's gone baby gone, already hurtling on the sweltering A to Jesus knows where and the neighbor lady comes out with her baby which she left sleeping in his bassinet and she's saying thank God. Thank you thank you thank you.

HOT DOGS

They were sweethearts. I was the interloper. Swan diving into their 4th of July barbeque. They knew I'd never learned to drive but hadn't offered a ride. Vitalized by two Bloody Marys, I'd called a cab. Walked into the Baldwin Hills mock-Tudor without knocking. Strode up to the groom in my fitted retro sundress and punched him on the arm. "I came for the celebs!" I cried, and I saw the bride cringe.

The newlyweds were playing at being settled and rich. The guy was an ex of mine. He'd availed himself of my instability, then took a powder when things got deep. He moved to Los Angeles. A year later, I pretended to have gotten a job here. Lulled him with fake normalcy. He and his new girl met me for dinner in West Hollywood and I'd gotten out without drinking, crying, or slandering anyone.

The now-wife's mother was a film reviewer for the Times. She was out of town leading a writers' retreat in an ice hotel somewhere.

I'd said that bit about celebs to be funny, since the guests had clearly left. But no; here one came, milky shoulders covered with a wrap. She was not the celebrity I'd come for. That one was shooting a movie with Harrison Ford.

"Bonnie? She had an early call," the groom said. Her name felt great in his mouth, I could tell. What a marvelous life he and his wife and mother-in-law were going to have.

The other celeb, the one who wasn't well known then but is very much so now, sat in the shade. She would only talk with the bride. The groom said to help myself to one of his mother-in-law's suits. I went inside, first stopping in the kitchen for two Coronas, which I drank bouncing on my rear on the mother-in-law's bed.

I found a black suit, very Bain du Soleil. Grabbed another beer on my way out. The celeb had vanished. The sun oozed down behind the backyard fence. The groom was playing "Taps" on a plastic recorder. I loved how boring he'd been. Boxes of sparklers sat on the main table's edge: they'd clearly hoped for their guests to stay longer. The bride's shoulders and arms rested on the pool's edge while her pale legs paddled.

"You skinny dip here?" I hollered over the sound of "Taps." In the corner of my eye, I registered that the groom had heard.

"Beautiful playing," came a voice from over the fence. We all looked. An older man, years of shouldered responsibility dragging his features down. Kilroy was here.

The groom aborted a guffaw and said thank you. The face disappeared.

"Are you kidding?" the bride asked me.

The groom gathered plates and bottles and hustled into the house. I was pretty drunk. A crazy woman is like catnip to a bore like him. I shucked the mother-in-law's suit. The bride met my gaze, shrugged herself free of hers. She lobbed it to a chair, where it landed with a dainty sucking sound. Flat-chested and sleek. Good for her.

We swam and chatted about nothing. The sultry weather. The Harrison Ford movie. Their honeymoon trip to Cabo. The light was perfect. I knew the groom was checking us out from inside.

My head hurt. Suddenly, I wanted to be dressed. But the dry suit wasn't where I'd left it at the pool's edge, and I hadn't thought of a towel. The bride's white teeth flashed. She'd thrown the suit when I wasn't looking.

I climbed out of the pool without regard for my curvy frame, my round and springy tits. Hoisted myself from the pool, perfectly lit.

THE OLD PAINTER

"The world's on fire and you're aaaaall talking about your inconsiderate roommates who are banging and then coming out afterward for fruit?" Behind him, the old painter has pinned a poster of his show from the Art Museum of Cincinnati. Even on my computer monitor, I can see that the corners of it are raggedy, as if he has moved the poster from apartment to apartment since the 1980s. The top right corner thumbtack drops and the poster curls.

I registered for this virtual painting class on a whim. For the occasion, I have gathered paper, a mug of water, and a drugstore toy section watercolor set. I wanted something to say that I did this weekend during the virtual team check-in at work Monday morning. This class was free to register; you give via Venmo at the end, and it's optional.

Most participants are muted, but the old painter's assistants' mics are live. That's how the teacher knows what they were talking about before he signed in. "I'm just saying, it's hilarious that before class started, everyone was talking about Pride Week as if it is even a thing right now when civilization is ending." His faded hoodie is tight across his belly, bunched at the armpits.

"What do you think about the way it's 112 degrees in Portland, Oregon today?" he continues. "How about the way we are all gonna die, like really, really soon?" The assistants, clearly stoned, laugh politely and in one case, manically.

There is a silence. Someone asks in the chat when we will start painting. The painter flashes a hand. "Wait!" He is angry at people who want to start. There are only 16 people total in the Zoom "gallery." You can see who is muted and who is not. So, only a handful who might end up paying something. A few shake their heads and their gallery boxes disappear. The old painter seems not to notice this. "I'm getting aggravated by you people laughing. You're inter-fucking-rupting my thoughts."

The old painter sighs. He has terrible teeth. "Okay, sorry to be a downer. Let's start again," he says. I am overdressed. I wonder how quickly I can turn my video off, change clothes, and get back on camera without being singled out.

"SAY! What's better than a re-tweet?" the painter asks. "Love? Pssh. Love fades. Love flees. But—hear me out—you might come home from being told you are in Stage IV cancer!" His eyes are bright. "Huh? HUH?"

The painter stands, wiping his mouth. He sighs. "Oh, right; so you might come home from the hospital with this terrible news and find that your Instagram post has been hearted 300 times and people are tagging their friends in it. Then you'll say, 'Hey, I just know I'll be in remission soon!'"

More gallery boxes wink out. The old painter reassures us that he is funny when he wants to be but opines that none of us burnouts really want that.

I am not stoned. When he asks us all to take a moment and regard his face, I do it. I am overwhelmed to behold in closeup the face of someone I do not know, someone who—because he has finally located his monitor's camera—is talking directly to me. "This is the face of someone who has lived," the old painter says softly. His eyes must have been pretty once. I register within me his long years of struggle and joy and pain. Will he ask us to paint him? "And folks, since the pandemic, my erections have been a-maaazing." Some of the participants' eyes dart in the way of people who are not sure they are hearing what they think they heard. I recognize this kind of eye darting.

"Fuck yeah!" The assistant laughs her crazy laugh again. I am grateful for her. Her voice and terrible laugh create a buffer I'm not sure I can remain here without. Especially now that the old painter is telling us that his parents wanted him to be an orthodontist, yet never got him braces for his own teeth. This is why, if we were together in person, we would now be wiping droplets of spittle off our chests, as he needs to wipe it from his computer screen now, he says.

The next question is one of those "more of a comment" ones and it's from another of the assistants, a straight-haired woman in one of those band t-shirts from which the neck-hole has been scissored out. "I'll show my tits if Venmos reach five hundred bucks."

Silence. The gallery faces are unmoving now.

"I mean, what the hell; my kids are asleep upstairs."

The painter looks disappointed, but also expectant. I am really let down. I want to message this woman that she is as good as anyone here. Most of the gallery faces look amused with a sprinkling of effort to appear nonchalant. It is an excruciatingly awkward moment, and yet it is one of human connection.

Finally, the old painter finishes rubbing his face and mutters that being stylish is important and that his wool cabbie cap is something he does for all of us. Then he says he is tired and must bid us all adieu. The faces wink out.

My finger hovers above the red LEAVE button. But I don't Leave. Now it is just me and the painter and the assistant who has offered to show her tits. I realize the old painter doesn't know how to click off.

There will be plenty of time to paint after this. A lifetime, in fact. But we won't be together like this, ever again. The assistant raises her top over her face and I press my open mouth to the screen, and under my lips bloom beautiful tiny rainbow-hued circles and circles and circles.

OVER THERE

Charles is my blood and what he feels, I feel. From the overhead vent, a soft breeze cools the sweat of his neck. I experience the small blessing of it, seeing him lean soft arms onto the checkout counter. My brother is dressed in the same black suit he wears to all our dinners. Charles is baldheaded like me, although my bony pate is covered—in the way of middle-aged men and ball players like the young Turk I saw near the refrigerator section of this CVS—in a ball cap.

The cashier assumes my brother and I are strangers. It is true we haven't greeted each other. Before him on the counter is a cheap, lime-green phone charger. It's clear he's been here a while. The cashier beckons me to the second register. Charles regards the charger.

"What happened?" I call over. The cashier is ringing up my eggs, bacon, and bottle of wine. I am using CVS as my market. Also, my bank. I press the buttons that add $20 "cash back" to my tab.

"My charger! I just bought it this morning." my brother says, looking past my face. "It was stolen. From the coffee shop!"

"Your phone charger was stolen?" Now it comes to me: my brother's smell. The greasy suit, the unwashed hair.

A small line is forming. The cashier gives a little huff. "I told you, sir, it's about $11.95 with tax," she tells Charles. I am alert to the small note of irritation. It isn't often I am witness to my brother's lived and public days.

"Are you at the shelter over near the church?" I continue, sliding my card back into my wallet. The cashier shakes her head slightly. She wears those gigantic, bamboo-style gold hoops that were popular twenty years ago or so. The kind that have to be hollow, or they'd be dragging down her lobes.

I know our conversation can wait. Charles and I are meeting for an early dinner. It's just happenstance we're both here at CVS across the parking lot from the coffee shop where apparently Charles spent at least part of the afternoon.

I've bought the wine, the breakfast supplies as a kind of reward for myself, I guess. A way to recognize my immense humanitarianism, meeting my brother at a neutral location to buy him a patty melt and some coffee which he'll ask to have refilled at least five times before we shake hands goodbye. My big brother also smells of urine; who wouldn't?

"Could you—" the cashier gestures to the line.

"I think he's next," I say, leaning over to palm Charles the twenty. My brother gives a brusque nod. Passes wind. Isn't it the strangest thing, how a person's farts can smell exactly the same after the years and miles and the horribly timed breakdowns?

"Yeah, no; The Berkeley Shelter. Took the bus." He flashes the flip phone as if to show the cashier, me, and the line of tired workers who are waiting that he does have a machine to be enlivened by the charger. I start for the door.

"Gotta have a phone," says the young Turk in the baseball uniform. Kindly, I want to believe. I startle when the glass door emits its electronic chime. My brother is the first to guffaw.

"Yo, Charles," I call back to my brother. He gives me a little half-salute that was a thing of his in high school. Our yearbook mentions it under his photo. "I'll see you over there, man."

I have a couple of minutes to pop my trunk and deposit my bounty. Wine to soothe me after our visit. I'll empty the bottle, imagining my brother telling the bus driver, then his dorm-mates at the shelter about his brother hooking him up with a brand-new charger and a princely meal. All the coffee he wanted.

I'll still be thinking of him when I awaken in the morning, temples thumping and gauze-mouthed. I'll think of my brother's half-salute as I fry up my bacon and eggs, grease seeping into my clothes.

LITTLE WILL

Will was born as a little friend for his mother. His scorched hometown was the site of an oil boom and the murder capital of the country.

His sisters had married and been carried off to make homes in Houston, in St. Louis, in Knoxville, Tennessee with the earnest and citrus-smelling men they'd ensnared.

The wildcatter's kids would bully Will for his blonde curls, his soft life. To make it up to him, his doctor father bought him a Shetland pony. He wasn't allowed to tell.

His father turned away a silver miner and his family because they couldn't pay. The family staged a protest where they walked on their knees to Will's dad's practice. The local paper sent a pimpled high school student who'd been hounding them for an assignment. The receptionist had cried and been fired.

In the mornings after his father strode down the walk with his leather satchel, Will would cry to stay home, and his mother would give in. He wasn't allowed to tell.

A handful of ladies would arrive for luncheon. Taking in the interior of the doctor's house for gossip and speculation, later. They all knew what his mother didn't: that little Will was curled under the table with a fistful of lemon cookies. Filled by the women's most intimate scents, and the sight of their restless legs. Spectator pumps lined up alongside stockinged feet.

One wore bracelets that tinkled prettily. Another had daubed an earthy scent behind her knees. A transporting sight: the metal clip that secured a stocking to a flesh-toned panty girdle. He experienced his first erections there, gnawing on sweetness. His whole life, he'd prefer older women.

. . . AND TITLE IT, "FAITH"

There's a beach. Mexico. A young couple in a convertible, winding up a coast. A couple so attractive their grim mouths add to their allure. The man's crucifix flashes in the sun. *Introduce the players—not too many—in media res.*

There is me, in Philadelphia. At this age, I look best in a turtleneck; white cotton in spring and summer; black wool in autumn and winter. A crucifix matching my son's. I'm a bookkeeper for a psychiatry practice. He worked through them one by one and pronounced them all imbeciles. A single mother, I couldn't afford to quit.

Already, the reader wants to return to Mexico with the handsome couple with their sunglasses and bright citrus smell. Okay. They pull over, and buy fish from a teenage boy under a *jalapa*. My son and his lover have been in Mexico long enough for the leather to relax, the tread of their sandals to shallow, their feet to darken.

What do they want? My son wants adventure. Takes a risk: invites the fish seller to join them in their hotel room. My son is in the unpredictable phase where his breath comes fast and his teeth flash.

His new girlfriend wants this to last and last. Her eyes are gray-green as the Pacific. She cannot believe her good fortune. She has money, but she never had such an exciting man desire her. She enjoys my son ordering her around; dismissing her when he fancies a solo beach run or to investigate something in town.

That is, show them, and make clear their problem. My son's most recent bout with depression left him pale and 70 pounds heavier. Barely able to make eye contact or speak, except to me. He lost the glamorous job he scored while still gold-tongued and charming.

The light, the smell of our home changed. I began stopping after work for a scotch mist or two before our night of television viewing.

Then, the pivot. His voice quickened. He lost the weight, tanned up, and hit the bars. Showered, shaved. He met the rich young woman he charmed into a Mexico adventure. Into breaking her lease and <u>LIVE</u>, why don't you?

In Mexico, there will be *foreshadowing*, inevitable in hindsight. Like my son's spending jags and all-night soliloquies. The lurid lines on his tendon-y neck, scored by the edge of that crucifix under flickering bathroom light.

That nice young woman will believe I never liked her.

I neither liked nor disliked. I needed for her to be up to the task. I was worn to a dried curl. I needed to hand my beautiful boy over for a week, a year, the rest of our lives. I wore my crucifix on the outside of my neck on a chain. An expression of my faith.

After Mexico was curtailed, the young woman brought my son home to me.

A decade later, beside her sleeping spouse, she will miss my son with an ache under her sternum that makes her cry out. She will touch herself and weep.

I miss my boy, too. My fiery toddler with his shock of curls. The remorseful teen who left a gold crucifix on my nightstand. Came to breakfast wearing an identical cross on a chain. The silent man who watched as I scored my own neck

with the metal cross one night while drunk—the reason I wear
turtlenecks.

What has changed?

I lie awake, too. In his room, my son snores. That always
happens when he gains so much weight.

I love him. I do not know how I want this to *end*.

ANTHROPOLOGY

The only job I could get after college was a temp gig at an oil firm in Century City, which looked the way most people picture Los Angeles. Sharp edges. White sky. Manicured palms.

I was an anomaly, with my anthropology degree and dangly Peruvian earrings. My first day, I tuned in to Anita Hill's testimony on KCRW. My cubicle-mate opined loudly that Hill was lying to get attention. The receptionist called it a "black-on-black" issue. Said we'd never know the truth.

"We do good work!" announced a faded banner in the break room. It was left over from a Chamber of Commerce ribbon-cutting when the firm moved in.

My boss, Jean, occupied a corner office. She had a stunning view across Santa Monica Boulevard: the emerald expanse of Los Angeles Country Club links. I'm not sure what Jean did at the firm. She always referred to herself as a top executive. She wore reading glasses on a beaded chain around her neck. Sometimes she'd arrive at work with bits of scrambled egg or toast crumbs on the small shelf her glasses made. I'd tip her off with a raised eyebrow and inclined head. I soon learned she was the founder's sister.

Every month, Jean used her expense account to treat us both to dinner at a swanky restaurant. We'd talk about basketball and get shitfaced on the house red. Her rudeness to the waiters was clearly her imitation of top executive behavior. Jean had terrible eyesight, so I had to read her the menu.

The founder drove Jean to and from work each day. But on the nights of these expensive dinners, I'd get her home to her place near Mount Saint Mary's, in the hills off the 405.

My own apartment was a ground-floor studio in shabby Culver City. All night long, shopping carts rattled past my bedroom window. On my block, an old man lived in the ivy beside the elementary school fence. His hair and flowing beard were the color of the sidewalk. His cerulean eyes stared from behind the bank of ivy like something from a fairy tale.

On my lunch hour, I'd escape the heat in the lobby of the Beverly Hilton or in Robinsons-May, where I once saw John Travolta buying socks. But most days, I'd take my solitary lunch to the fancy outdoor mall splashed with giant yellow umbrellas. To reach it, you crossed over a concrete bridge over Avenue of the Stars.

The all-male committee concluded their hearing. Anita Hill's testimony had fallen on deaf—no, disdainful—ears. Minds that couldn't conceive of blocking a Supreme Court appointee because of the way he'd treated a woman. At work, I heard applause erupt from the conference room.

All I wanted to do was go home to my bed. But it was time for one of those fancy dinners with my boss.

Jean favored the kind of place with obsequious waiters who pulled out our chairs and used a crumb scraper after we laid waste to the bread. Before we ordered, Jean delivered the news: she was getting a radical mastectomy. I knew she'd been out a lot, but this was the first I'd heard of any of this. In the solipsism of youth, I simply hadn't noticed.

Jean's face was illumined by the small table lamp. She looked wan and almost pretty. Instead of wine, we ordered apple martinis. I wanted to bring up the topic of Clarence Thomas—surely not everyone at work thought Anita Hill was lying—but what was the point? If Jean agreed with the rest of them, I'd feel more alone than ever. Her watery eyes were taking in the dessert cart.

Outside in the cold, I realized I was seriously drunk. On the way to Jean's, I careened around corners, twice scraping my bumper. I stopped for gas and nearly drove away with the gas spigot still jammed into the tank. Under the eye-smarting light, Jean dozed, her mouth slightly open. Unguarded. I saw how she must have looked as a child. How she would look as an elderly woman, if she were allowed that.

Jean lived in an old house off Mulholland, atop a winding hill. In front, a streetlight flickered. A coyote howled. Jean roused herself to say they got pretty loud out there sometimes. She made no move to leave. It was getting late. I still had the drive home. I mumbled something about being sorry about her cancer and to let me know if there was anything I could do.

"Well. I'm not a young woman, and of course, not married. Still, it would be nice if someone said goodbye."

That was when she did it. Pulled up her sweater, her blouse. Her bra went with them under her soft chin.

I leaned forward and placed my cheek against her breast. I set my palm against the other. Her body was the same temperature as the inside of my car. She smelled lightly of baby powder.

We sat there for some moments. Jean swallowed once, but that was it. Then she straightened her clothing, exited the car, and started up the walk.

I remember nothing about the drive back to Culver City. But I recall how it felt to awaken hours later with my apartment lights blazing, door ajar. My car keys dangling from the lock. The sound of my jangling phone. It was my temp office, calling to inform me my gig at the oil firm was over. Later that day, I'd find Jean's shoes on the passenger side floor of my car. I kept them there for months.

I sometimes think of Jean in her house on the top of that dark hill off Mulholland Drive. Surrounded by slinking coyotes. Below, the mushrooming ranks of unsheltered people and celebrities and top executives and young folks trying on adulthood.

I don't live in L.A. anymore, but I sometimes travel there. When the descent into LAX begins, a vast golden grid of light is splayed out below. Closer, backyard pools face heavenward, sightless as martyred saints.

THREE WAYS: A TRIPTYCH OF LOVE AND ITS IMPRINT

Haight Street the Night Before, on the Back of Roma's Harley

Nick Sweet is riding sidesaddle in a cotton-candy Marilyn wig and flecked wiggle dress. The black air perfumed with night-blooming jasmine. When Roma kills the engine, it seems the world has ended; it is that glass-ly quiet. On a sloped lawn in Golden Gate Park, she works his neck raw with her teeth and cat's tongue.

Now it is the next day. Nick is freshly showered in jeans and flannel shirt, Greyhound-bound back home to San Pedro. He chats with a spirited pre-teen who reminds him of his niece. Her parents are clearly relieved a polite adult is taking an interest. Every half hour, Nick excuses himself for the clattering metal restroom, where he removes a loafer, scrapes cherry polish from another nail. Each time he pulls on a toe, it emits a small pop.

It Added Up; It Just Didn't Work

After her boyfriend dumped her, Azucena chose a painter, mournful and louche. He spoke French and had Cat Stevens' eyes, George Harrison's soft handlebar. He rolled his own cigarettes with fingerless gloves. This was Azucena's version of "I'm Gonna Wash That Man Right Outta My Hair."

The painter visited her at the Film Arts Foundation, where she was editing a friend's film. The film was a documentary about vibrators. He pushed her down onto the couch. Azucena kicked. "I'll scream," she swore. He ascertained otherwise. He slipped his fingers into her mouth, knowing she would not bite. She let him do it. She just couldn't bear to think of herself as a victim. The man was simply a mediocre carnivore, with a musky aura of tobacco and amber resin.

"I'm not in a place for something serious," he told her afterward. In French. Those eyes. Azucena was unmoved. Only frustrated that her strategy was unsuccessful. She yearned more than ever for her mechanic ex-boyfriend. His musky underpinnings, those battered hands on her skin, marking her with the scent of motor oil.

We Were at It Again

Richard's mother was a pageboy-coiffed, Panama hat-wearing woman. A leading player on the community theater scene. Now she was single, working as always in the office of the elementary school around the corner from their house.

His dad had gone without a word to his son. He'd taken only the framed Lautrec print, which we'd replaced with a Scrabble board with risqué words glued on and a thrift-store painting of a wolf.

Richard and I were hired to paint his mother's bedroom and organize her shoes. We finished one coat. We shot a Polaroid picture of every pair of shoes, then affixed the photos to the outward-facing side of each shoebox.

Then we sat shoulder to shoulder on his mother's soft bed. I touched the spray of lavender paint in Richard's hair, then slipped my hand inside his shirt. He ducked his head and kissed me on the cheek. "We'd better get back to it," he said.

At three, we were finished. We celebrated with ice-cream-and-schnapps shakes. I found a strappy orange sundress in the closet. The last Polaroid is of me, slit-eyed and moue-ing. I remember the moment Richard snapped it. The soft punch and whir of the camera. The way, under the camera's lens, Richard's sweeter lips imitated mine.

THE ANGLE OF DEPRESSION

Mignon, as always, wants to know what I'm thinking. I have finally agreed to meet her in person, at the Berkeley Art Museum. The new one, with its blinding white walls and tomato-hued interior doors and echoey stairwells. A café with wine and salads of watermelon and feta and mint.

"Meat space," Mignon called it.

But by the time we finish viewing the Peter Hujar photos in the lower gallery, I've formed the view that no one, ever, should visit an art museum in the company of another person. I want to scream in the metal stairwell.

Yet here we sit in the museum café, emptied splits of champagne before us. It's hot and my hair is heavy, redolent with horsey-smelling henna. Everyone else is in camisoles and shorts in ice cream colors. Last night I did my hair—yes, for "the occasion"—and it came out too bright.

"I liked the photos of the wrecked cars," I say in answer to Mignon's question. "And that glum guy with the giant penis." What I am hollering inside is what I am always silently screaming at museums. "You don't know me! You don't know my taste!" Under the table, I rev my roller skates.

I met Mignon online. Our exchanges have been filled with nuance and shy disclosures. Once, I offered the details of a violent crime of which I'd been a victim. Mignon confessed she'd once driven into a kid on a bike. Another time, we'd negotiated logging off to cry, after confessing to each other the depth of our loneliness.

But in person, Mignon emits a river of combat and insecurity, just like everyone else around here. What band/bistro/hiking trail am I obsessed with, that no one else has heard of? Who eats the local-est, grass-fed-est food? Who's vacationed in the farthest-flung place?

I gaze out the window at the office supply store across the street, with its industrial carpeting, balm of greenish light and wide aisles.

"It's slightly annoying how Hujar framed his subject in the center of the shot," I say.

Mignon brightens, pouring the remaining bubbly into her flute. "He learned a way of composing called the Angle of Depression," she explains, eyebrows raised self-importantly. "See, it's the idea that the viewer's eye takes this angle—well, technically, this diagonal line ends below the bottom edge. There's something we don't see."

She continues, telling me how Hujar's last name would be pronounced in Spanish, if he were Spanish, which he probably is. How the British television show, The Office, was modeled after a David Foster Wallace story about working for the IRS. Tongue loosened by drink, she adds that she puts away a bottle of wine every night before opening her laptop to see if I've written.

She meets my eyes then. She picks up a ball of melon and tucks it into her mouth. Meaningfully, it appears.

"Will you excuse me?" I said, then glide to the women's room. A pullover youth with pimples around their mouth enters behind me.

Determined to act casual, I attempt a "selfie" in the bathroom mirror. My russet hair smolders nicely in the recessed lights. But then my bag slips into the sink, setting off the automatic gush from the faucet. My legs fly from under me. Fucking hell!

I consider staying down for a day or so. Who would know, other than half-in-the-bag Mignon and now this waif currently attempting to exit their stall.

"Hi! Help!" I say, rolling aside. The waif's sweater as they easily lift me smells of fabric softener.

They ask if I'm all right. "You betcha!" I cry, and the waif toddles off.

I skate back and gingerly settle. I feel like I'd been attacked by a javelina. My flank throbs. I swear to fucking god the infant is coming back with a fresh split of sparkling wine.

"You know him?" Mignon asks. "He's so . . . frat."

"No frat boy uses Downy."

"You have an awesome day, ma'am," the waif says, their mouth a hard line.

Why did I wear these ridiculous skates? And why does this pain feel deserved?

Mignon snaps her fingers, as if an idea has occurred to her, or maybe just to capture my attention. How long have I had my nose pierced? Because she recently removed her nipple ring, which she got in her thirties "because of National Geographic."

"I could give it to you!" she says. "I just have the one . . ."

"Oh! I guess I always thought they came in twos, like earrings. Or, you know, none," I say.

". . . although I have been wondering how much I could get for it, like, at a We Pay Cash for Gold place."

Meat space. Who needs it?

Let's say I summon the courage of my convictions. Soothe myself by purchasing pencils and notebooks across the street. A squishy wrist strip to subdue my carpal tunnels.

Or more dramatically, I could emulate the mountain lion in that recent news story. Remember? The one where the two cyclists did all the things we're told to do: holler real loud, make themselves appear larger. If I could be that magnificent beast, I'd rake Mignon with my claws and spare the pimpled waif to spread the tale.

But that isn't the way the story went. Remember?

In real life, it was an elderly couple. The lady neutralized the mountain lion by jabbing it in the eyes with her ballpoint pen. She saved herself and her mate.

See, in the end, you can do everything you are supposed to do. But fate doesn't give a hoot. Me, Mignon, the cyclists. The mountain lion. The waif from the woman's room. Even beautiful Peter Hujar, with his portraits of the famous, the abject, the endowed. The ruined cars.

"I like people who dare," Hujar said. "Yet here we are frozen, cast in our living roles. I am lonely as hell, and that is no lie."

I split the sparkler between our two glasses and say to Mignon, "To me. And, you know, us."

BEFORE THE ELECTION

It is a hot Halloween in San Juan Bautista, California. The town is deserted. Three chickens high step out of the road as you turn onto the main street. The town grew up around the Mission, built in the early 1800s. The same mission where Jimmy Stewart followed Kim Novak up the spiral stairs to the high steeple. Obsessed. All those falls into open air, wild-eyed in bolts of bruised sky.

Like Judy in the movie, you are a fallen woman. At home, men follow you in their cars. They form and change you. They see themselves as rescuers. When the rescue attempts fail, you are left for the next one to dress and paint you up.

On Third Street, in front of Doña Esther's, you exit your car, pulling the back of your skirt away from damp flesh. Discarded pandemic masks are banked against the doors of the businesses, all closed.

An old man blocks the door of Doña Esther's. He is stooped and skinny. He wears a battered t-shirt that reads "THE FIRST AFRICAN AMERICAN PRESIDENT OF THE UNITED STATES."

Once he and you shared a feeling: excitement that Barack Obama had been elected president. President of the United States. But he is not the president now. He will not be the president again. The man regards your rumpled dress, your white go-go boots.

"What do you think you're doing?"

"I'm here for . . . the banquet. The Halloween puppets."
Afterward, you usually visit the mission to pay your respects to
the Mutson who were enslaved there. Then you cool off and
catch your breath in the wood and velvet sanctuary, under the
gazes of Spanish saints.

Jimmy Stewart has vertigo because of his guilty conscience.
A policeman died because of him. He throws himself into the
annihilation of height. A dreamed grave. The spiral hairdo of a
woman whose personality he erases. A woman who startles at
the sight of a nun, and plummets to her death.

The Vertigo Effect is achieved by zooming in fast, while
pulling the camera back at the same time. You also get this
feeling when you're old, when looking up can throw you off
kilter. Or when you observe an old man resting his hand on his
hip-sheathed knife. A leather sheath stamped with poppies. Like
those barrettes and hard purses they used to sell in Tijuana.

The door to Doña Esther's is locked. Earlier, you'd called.
You chalked up the unanswered phone to a busy lunch hour
and set off anyway. Inside, you see the arched interior doorways.
Long shadows streak the dining room's red walls. You register
the smell of something burning. Something that isn't food.

"What do you want?" you ask him.

"My teeth. My work. My family," he answers. "This
restaurant was supposed to be a polling place." This is a man
who has felt pride. Who once stood tall, with a strong and lively
skeleton inside. Worked. Sired boys and girls. Are they alive
now, these children?

Behind the man are the three chickens. They scratch and
murmur. Your boots are dulled with dust. The man is not as
old as you first thought. He has no fingernails, you notice,
zooming out and zooming in. He smells of sweat and lavender.
His t-shirt is stained with a red sauce. From inside Doña
Esther's comes the sound of a ringing phone. The bright echo

of those rings hangs in the hot air. You and the old man stand there together on the whirling earth, just below the San Andreas Fault. Around the two of you, the sky pulses purple.

During the Mission period, over 19,421 Native Americans died at Mission San Juan Bautista and approximately 150,000 Native Americans died in California.

CODPOD

My husband owed Codpod a favor. Or at least they both agreed that he did. Joe roared off right after dinner. I stood in the doorway and watched him take the corner. I was used to it.

Codpod and I had never met. He hadn't shown up at our wedding, even though he was supposed to be the best man.

Joe and Codpod were teens together in Fernley, Nevada. They met one blistering summer day on the cul-de-sac where they both lived. It seems Joe had stuck his dad's .22 out a second-floor window and was waving it around. Codpod—at least this was how I heard the story—carried on watering down his rock landscape. Everyone else had fled into their homes. Something in Codpod's casual stance struck Joe. Soothed him. He'd come down without the gun and talked quietly with Codpod until the sheriffs came. Codpod had saved my husband's life, probably.

I told you I've never met him, and it's true. But this morning we received a wedding gift, delivered in person by one of Cod's ex-wives. She was statuesque in white shorts and a spangly halter top. Fusilli curls. Inside the cardboard box she bore was a beautiful cat, a Russian Blue. She couldn't stay, she said, flashing a smile. Her accent was also Russian. She wore braces on her teeth. As she dipped down into the driver-side seat, I saw that she had the roundest rear end I'd ever seen.

"Did you see that?" Joe asked me without moving his lips after he'd helped her close the car door.

"You mean, this isn't a dream?" There we stood with our box of cat, in front of a building that allowed no pets. We hustled her inside and named her Lola.

It would be nice to have a little friend. Joe was gone so much. But all day, Lola just hunkered behind our cinderblock and board bookshelves. When we left her alone and returned, her bowls were clean.

"This is trauma," Joe explained, his brows lowered in the way they always did when he was teaching me something. "This is what a traumatized cat looks like, Letty."

It was warm, and I'd left our unscreened front windows open to catch the breeze. It was four hours from Oakland to Reno, and Codpod's place in Fernley was 50 miles past that. But now it was 2 a.m. and there had been no call. The black hole inside me stretched, widened. That old familiar feeling. Like the Grand Canyon in its terrifying fullness of emptiness, if you know what I mean.

Meanwhile, Lola's bowls were still filled. She wasn't behind the bookshelves or in the bathroom, where the litter box was. Joe should have called by now. And now Lola was missing? My pulse skittered. I took a shaky breath and phoned Codpod.

"Good evening, Letty," he said as though we spoke at two every morning. No, Joe hadn't shown up. Codpod sounded a little testy. Maybe Joe had stopped in Reno for a few hands, or a slice of pie.

Joe never would have stopped in Reno. He'd been in a little trouble there, right before we met. I asked Codpod to have Joe call me when he got in. Or if, you know, he heard anything.

"And vicey versey," he returned, and we said our good nights. I cradled the unused litter box, feeling like I was curled at the edge of one of those terrifying sinkholes you hear about in the desert or in South America.

I was awakened by our upstairs neighbors having sex. They were a young couple. The guy stayed home all day in his faded rock band t-shirts, blasting Snoop Dog. His girlfriend was a plump Latina who left every day at eight in pumps and a suit.

Now I was completely alone in this cheap apartment where mold framed the windows and smeared the walls below them. My new husband: vanished in the Nevada desert. What would I do without him? Plus, my new cat had taken a powder as soon as she had the chance. I dropped to my knees, sobbing. "I can't bear it," I whimpered.

As if in answer, the woman upstairs wailed.

The telephone jangled. It was Joe. He sounded excited.

It seemed he'd had second thoughts about that favor he owed Codpod. True, Codpod had something on him, he explained. But he'd rather call Cod's bluff than continue his association with that bad apple. He had me to consider now.

That's what he said: Continue his Association. Bad Apple. He Had Me.

Pure devotion flooded my chest. Ok! Ok! I yelled. He wanted me to know everything, he hollered back. Because he was mine and I was his. One hundred percent.

My Joe! I couldn't wait to see him again. I didn't care where he'd been, or what Codpod had on him. I'd trade that for having Joe back home. *Our* association would continue. I had him. He would help me find our wild kitty so we could raise and tame her and spend peaceful evenings all together in our tiny home.

My flyer had a picture of Lola and the words: HELP ME. I'd forgotten to include our telephone number. Joe was in it after all because he was the one holding her. His eyes were so warm, so kind. They contained the key, I just knew to my future.

FLUX

I. On a Sleepless Night, Your Slumbering Wife Beside You

Do you ever think about how your friend from the film department introduced us after the Vertigo screening, how I started calling you late at the adult theater you managed, and how you'd chat with me between ticket sales? Ever think about the night I visited you at your apartment and met your Russian housemates? How someone brought out firecrackers, and I made a dumb joke about calling the police and was met with those hard stares? How you drank too much and started nuzzling me and how you said beer made you frisky? How we went to your room, and you said I shouldn't mention the police because of the firearms in the house? How you told me you were a professional typist and played me the outgoing voicemail message and it was a funny take on your business name, "Finger King," that had out-of-work pianists pounding out final papers for students from USF and the medical school? How you'd brought a six-pack into your room, and how we started fooling around how you couldn't get it up, and how just before you passed out I asked for cab fare and you gestured to your wallet and how all it contained was your driver's license—I was suspicious enough to check your weird last name but there it was on the government document—and some expired coupons for cat food? How a few days later I got you to come to my apartment and you couldn't get it up and I asked if it was me

43

and you said, not in a million years, and made me orgasm with your fingers? And how I let all this happen even though (this, a decade before 9/11), you'd shown me a children's book you wrote in which the main character is a big hero for identifying a suspicious man in a turban on a flight? And how you, carless like me, accompanied me on the airport shuttle when I was visiting my folks? And how we got there early and started drinking beer and kissing and how I missed the plane even though we were sitting in the waiting area right in front of the boarding gate? And how you ghosted me for real after I returned, and I obsessively called your number from pay phones all over San Francisco? Remember how you kept that stupid Finger King/Pianist message on? And how, one rainy night in front of the Opera House, I called you one last time and your outgoing message was clearly meant for your girlfriend, who had a Catholic-sounding name like Mary Theresa or Katherine Anne? How you pleaded with her weeping *in your outgoing voicemail message* to give you another chance? How you swore I was just a lost soul whom you'd helped at school and who wouldn't stop calling you and how you promised you were still pure for her, Mary Tess?

II. The Finger King's Best Times Are Behind Him

In his salad days, he'd studied literature at San Francisco City College. His professors had been encouraging, especially once they heard he managed an adult movie theater on Market Street and that he'd met Hunter S. Thompson, then famously serving as the night manager at the Mitchell Brothers Theater on O'Farrell.

The Finger King had been a big drinker, mainly beer or vodka shots out on the patio with his Russian roommates or every night alone in his room. He had a girl back home, a

Catholic girl who was saving herself for marriage. That was okay with the Finger King. He'd save himself, too.

He practiced on girls from the theater or film department. Grew adept at eliciting orgasms using neither his penis nor his mouth. The joke was that The Finger King was also the name of his business. He was a nimble typist, and prepared papers for other students. Word got around. As he typed, he couldn't help but make improvements.

Every month, he'd take the Greyhound Bus back home to Santa Barbara. First church, then brunch with the old widower and of course Mary Theresa. "I'll leave you kids to visit," the old man would say afterward and retire to his room for a lie-down. The Finger King and Mary Theresa would kiss and watch The Wide World of Sports.

The Finger King grew up without a mother. This drew a certain kind of woman to him and would for most of his life. One such woman, 12 years his senior, became his wife and the mother of his children. He'd married a wealthy woman. He thinks of those adult theater days as his misspent youth. "But I sure had fun!" he always adds with a wink and a flashed grin before his mouth settles back into its slot-like default.

Now, driving alone down eye-5 after taking his daughter to college in Berkeley, he thinks of a blue-eyed gal from the film department and how she used to call him from telephone booths all over town. He never answered. He'd been so loyal to Mary Tess he'd never done anything with these girls but fool around a little.

He remembers that little blonde from the film department, with her dimples and sad eyes. The way she'd curl her body around him as he used his dexterous fingers on her. How he'd put her in a cab afterward and return to vodka and his typing. Maggie, was that it? Marnie? Suddenly, with the marriage and child-rearing part of his life behind him, it seems crucial for him to remember. He pulls over at San Juan Bautista, slowing for the road chickens, and paces the hushed flagstones of the mission, it nags at him so much. So tranquil, so old. The San Andreas Fault is just behind.

He could still become a monk. He thinks of that scene in Vertigo, where the sight of a nun startles Kim Novak and she falls from the steeple. That girl from college.

He'd had a cat back then, he thinks. He had, hadn't he?

LUCKY DAY

I'm a lucky bastard of scattered habits. My books are marked by ladies' underthings. They bring me tea and flowers and leave earrings in my bedclothes.

She is the best of them, honey hair and citrine eyes I daren't meet. At eight in the morning, I awake in a jumble of sheets. Slip out in the nick of time. Husbandly shouts emit like trumpet blasts from between window rails. The scent of her stays on my hands and mouth.

At ten o'clock I hear from friends: she's divorced. If I have some blame to shoulder, no one but me honey-headed her could connect the dots.

I hear she's fled: Ibiza. At noon I carry on in gray Astoria, under the 1964 bridge to the Great State of Washington. By two, I'm in Rock Springs, Wyoming. Riding to the trona mines with dirty-necked men in a busted down truck.

Four p.m. finds me on the downswing, an ordinary rector at a Rust Belt house of prayer. When I finish, the pews glow amber.

By six, I'm running sound at the Fort Worth opera house. When the lights dim, I feel a tug on my laces. I know not to meet those olive-lemon eyes. In a low postscript, she calls me a fraudulent work of art.

She performs her warbling singthing to wild acclaim. But before the curtain call, she's gone. I rise from my soundboard and fall to my knees. My knotted-together laces pile-drive me to carpet. I loosen my tie and reach for my comb.

Ten p.m. finds me walking the highway, graceless and bleary. Music caroms in my head. A black splash lashes my legs. Her and those eyes. She extends an invitation in Catalan. I meet citrine at last and arrive at a grateful rest.

I awake at midnight, ensnared and alone. Beyond the billowy curtain splays Lake Pontchartrain, with its talismanic ten-mile bridge. By one, I'm face down in estuary mud.

THE GAP YEAR

We were staying in Alan's son's cabin in Bondurant, Wyoming, 30 miles outside of Jackson. But once a week we'd drive into town. Our ritual was to hit the dump. Alan's squeaky Bronco would be ripe with the stink of our bagged trash. Then it was laundry and a bite to eat at the Million Dollar Cowboy Bar. Finally, we'd visit his three-acre parcel. Undeveloped, encircled by a buck rail fence, with a glorious view of the Tetons.

I was taking what richer families would later call a "gap year." For me, it was more of a "what would I study and how will I pay?" year. Or just a "what now?" year.

It began with a receptionist job at a big high-rise near the lake. But already I was jobless, living it up with my ex-boss like a rodeo queen, in Wyoming, U.S.A.

The same realtor who'd sold Harrison Ford his place also sold Alan his parcel. The story went that no one had wanted to help Ford, who'd arrived at the real estate office dusty and rank on a motorcycle. I wondered how old this story had to be—wasn't that first Star Wars a million years ago?—but Alan went for the bait and loved to repeat it.

I don't remember who started our ritual of peeing in the corners of Alan's lot. Of course, it was easier for him, being a man. One day I spied a porcupine balanced on the fence, half-hidden by a cottonwood's droop, and mistook it for a cat. Crouching there with my jeans and panties lowered and the smell of my own urine in my nostrils, I wondered sincerely whether it was true they could shoot their quills. "Funny little girl," Alan said when I told him, patting me on the back like a pal.

Alan had convinced me to quit my job and join him in Wyoming. I didn't need to worry about money, he said. So long as we stayed together, neither of us added. I hadn't loved the baleful looks and conversations that broke off when I entered the break room at work. It was an old story; a boss and his assistant. He was still the boss.

The dirt road where the parcel sat ended at the green and fast-moving Snake River. One day, we met a man on that road. He looked to be about Alan's age, but his face was doughy and sun-flushed. He said he and his wife had a newborn baby, and that they were the first to have built on their parcel. He told us the enormous spread across from him was owned by Larry Ellison from Oracle, two names that meant nothing to me. Alan straightened, impressed.

We were close enough to the river to hear its singing rush. The air was redolent with sagebrush and wild mint. Alan, standing feet wide apart, offered the man a look at his land. A tad eagerly, I thought. I knew how he felt because I'd felt it myself: as long as he owned the spot and did nothing with it, he was on equal terms with anyone. I begged off, saying I wanted to sit by the river. By the time they set off, the man had invited us to dinner.

I picked my way across the stones at the riverbank. It hadn't occurred to me there'd be no place to sit. I was in the presence of majesty, with the slate Tetons scraping the western sky. I lowered myself onto the sharp rocks and stayed there, even though it hurt. The water looked muscular, as if it could swell up and grab me, with only the jagged peaks as witness.

Our hostess was sweet, no older than I was. Her black hair and red lips made me think of Snow White. She told us that earlier, she'd taken the baby out and gathered red and orange leaves and pinecones to fashion the centerpiece. She also produced a meal of porterhouse steak, squash soup, a green salad, and freshly baked cookies. What had I done today? Given my lover a patient hand job, applied lipstick, and hopped into the Bronco for the ride to town. My ass was still tender from sitting on the rocky bank of the Snake.

I kept pace with our host, putting away glass after glass of red-black pinot noir. Alan requested and received beer. He told the story about Harrison Ford, and when asked, said that we'd met at work. With each new bottle of beer, the wife brought a fresh frosty mug.

Through a white plastic monitor came the sounds of the baby making its noises in another room, and the wife excused herself. Our host was beet-faced by this time. His eyes were slits. I thought he might be asleep. I wobbled into the hallway to find a bathroom. A door was halfway ajar and I pushed it. It was a bedroom for the baby. Inside, her infant in her arms, Snow White dozed. The baby regarded me with a grave expression. Neither of us blinked. Beside its flushed face, Snow White's nipple glistened.

Back in the dining room, I mimed to Alan that everyone was asleep, except for us and of course the baby. We expressed our thanks. Back home in Chicago, no one had ever invited Alan and me out as a couple. Alan lost all his friends in his divorce, and so far, his sons had refused to meet me.

To our surprise, the host roused himself, insisting on walking us to the road. Alan ambled ahead, humming. Our host put his forehead against mine and said that I was a real peach. "How old are you, anyway?" he said into my ear. He smelled pleasantly of sweat and alcohol and cigarettes. It made me think of my grandfather, but I knew enough not to say so.

After the short walk in the dark, Alan and I pitched our dusty tent and dragged our sleeping bags inside. Everything was spinning. I could hear Alan wandering and pissing and chuckling to himself. I worried momentarily that he'd fall. An accident or illness was the kind of thing that would skew our future. It would fall to me to care for him. It's as much of a plan as I had. It didn't mean I couldn't choose another plan. Just that I didn't have one.

In the tent, Alan dragged his wiry body over mine and soon I heard his untroubled breath. I rolled to the opening, in case I needed to throw up. Hours later, I awoke half in; half out. The crisp air was infused with an ammoniac tang.

Before Alan awoke, I cleaned myself up with the jugged water we kept in the Bronco. Under the passenger side wiper was a thick envelope. Inside was a colorful packet of wildflower seeds, with our hosts' names, an image of their smiling faces, and the date, a year prior. A keepsake from their wedding day. The text promised Lewis blue flax and yellow prairie coneflower. Red Mexican hat, sweet anise, and Rocky Mountain iris. Purple coneflower and California poppy. The words were like incantations against a blank future.

I began scattering the seeds. I sprinkled without burying, with no thought of how they'd receive water. Then I sat on the buck rail fence and regarded our land. I imagined it next year at this time, blanketed in a riot of color.

I MEAN, NORMAN!

I check my mouth in the bronze floor button panel. A nearly pink gloss with just a hint of shimmer. I fluff my hair, adjust my padded bra. The tiny elevator smells of bitter tea and unwashed hair.

It really is too dreary outside for a proper picnic. Mr. ______ and I have arranged our first date to take place in his office. And now we are face to face, breathing. Under my clothes, my heart skitters.

"Millie," he intones. "Welcome aboard." He is every bit as handsome as his photos, which is to say, medium.

I recognize insecurity when I see it. His eyes remain on mine a fraction too long. He needs to know what I think. His big secret is that he cares. A former fatty, like me. In fact, we have texted about this. Caring too much. This fact is like catnip to an empath like myself. An INFP on the Myers-Briggs type indicator.

"Normal; I mean, Norman." Our little joke. I give him my hand. Our skin is moisturized and slightly sweaty.

Now, faces appear from behind cubicle walls. The women he supervises. "My kinkdom," he texted last night. Just his harmless way. He can be so corny! He has also said he utilizes one of those hotel desk bells and given each of his ladies a code. One ding for Recruitment. Two for Retention. And so on.

One gives a raised-brow nod and says hi. Her makeup covers pocked skin. This is Turnover. Mr. _______ has told me he and Turnover have a hilarious game they play. When one of them is away from their desk, the other strews three-hole-punch confetti over the vacated space.

I am not saying I like Mr. ______. It's too soon for his qualities to begin morphing from those of a stranger to someone I have ahold of, someone to pin a dream or two upon. But online dating has depleted me. It is down to this. A promise of a gluten-free vegetarian lunch behind the closed door of Mr. ______'s office, surrounded by Star Trek figurines and plaques from the Chamber of Commerce.

I glance at his open office door. Our deteriorating bodies are replete with the yearning and hopefulness of youth. For this date, I have sprung for a turquoise bra and panties set. I have told Mr. ______ about this and know his pulse is dancing now because I know Mr. ______ in the way we can know someone who has virtually shared raw facts and data in a way they never would, face to face over a date or two.

The idea that I have the power to make a pulse dance is a bit of a thrill. He knows about the smooth flesh where my breasts once stood. I have described the tattoo—a rolling field of California poppies— with which I was gifted last year at the Ink Kings tattoo competition in Sacramento. He has said he wants to see it, setting my own pulse shimmying.

But we're not there yet. Recruitment, Retention, and Turnover are gathering their purses, are wishing us a nice lunch. I do not know these women, but I hope they see me as a keeper.

Maybe we will be friends. Mr. _____ beams, pans his gaze. Like a bouquet of lollies in every flavor, exactly as he has said.

17 REASONS WHY

Late last night, Engine 22 got a call. For a moment, Chela, Leticia, and I were alone at the firehouse kitchen table. Chela stood, snapped: Up! Outside, we sat on the sidewalk against the building. Watched them leave us, sirens wailing. Then the metal door rolled shut and it was quiet again. When they returned, they sent us to Berkeley for more coke.

Now it is morning, but barely. I am jittering on a couch at Chela's. The cable car tracks are singing, sewing alarm into my pulse: Shame! Shame! Shame! I am jittering on a couch at Chela's. Her man is a firefighter. Chinatown native. Small-time coke dealer. He's still on duty around the corner. Sunlight hints, pink and yellow. I need to be in the office by eight. My body feels scraped hollow. My eyes are like cocktail onions.

Chela is the one who talked me into this punk haircut and dye job, these pointy Joe Jackson shoes. She calls me "Nat," for Natalie Wood. Chela and I work together at an office on Montgomery Street. Last week, I took magic mushrooms while the rest attended an industry luncheon. I wasn't allowed, since I'm not old enough to drink wine. While they sipped, I lay on the founder's cheese-colored leather couch and watched his *amate* paintings squirm.

I am always ill at ease here at Chela's. Ever since that one time one of the firefighters, off duty, came in drunk for a visit and chased me around the glass coffee table. Everyone laughed their asses off. I kept thinking someone would help me.

I stagger barefoot into Chela's kitchen, pop open a can of Coke. Only it isn't a Coke; the can is a headshop safe with a tight roll of bills inside. Will Chela's boyfriend count the bills to see if I stole?

The firefighters think I am a sharp cookie, which compared to Chela and her sister Leticia, I guess I am. Leticia is pregnant, but no one is supposed to know.

The fire captain, Marshall Nugent, likes me. He slips me valium, so I have a fighting chance at sleep. Once he took me to his place in Marin County. He refers to San Francisco as a ghetto, and Donald Trump as a real American. Sometimes late, he'll come by my place to see if I'm up. One time, he visited me at work in the Financial District and took me to lunch. He wore an unfashionable wide tie and brown shoes. At Station 22, only Chela's boyfriend is single.

I have to go to work. I splash my mouth and face, locate my Joe Jackson shoes and carry them down the stairs and onto the apartment building's stoop. The fog is a balm.

On my way to the bank today, someone will urge me to smile. I may do so at the teller window, depositing all that cash I stole from Chela's man.

I'M IN YOU

It was 1976, America's bicentennial year. Skylab, the first US space station, had orbited Earth for too long and was failing. The airwaves were filled with angel-headed Peter Frampton, with his wah-wah voice box and fake audience members losing their shit.

On the community theater scene, Nidia and I were not kids but not legal, either. Jailbait, they called us. Nidia and I wore our tightest pants with platform shoes. She knew these people because her parents acted in this theater before they divorced.

For after-show parties, we'd wear polyester halter dresses we bought in downtown San Pedro from Travis, an old man in a greasy fedora. Through the part on the dressing room fabric Travis watched us try the dresses. We didn't care. We zipped one another up, filling the tiny shop with the scent of Herbal Essences and Love's Baby Soft.

The bar around the corner from the community theater was called the Branch Office. Nidia and I would cage ginger ales and little bags of potato chips and clung to unemployed, middle-aged men on the dance floor, driving them wild.

Sure, Nidia and I were jailbait. But we were safe. These grown men put their dicks in our curious hands and said they could go to jail for what they wished they could do. But they were friends of Nidia's parents. When they asked if they could finish and we said no, they stopped. Excused themselves and returned with their pants done up.

Like Benny Sher, a Cajun teetotaler from New Orleans. The wide front seat of his white Cadillac reclined with a purring sound. He begged to watch me touch myself. His backseat teemed with empty cans of Near Beer. His fiancée managed a bank.

I loved that my body—the one the boys at school ignored—could render grown men helpless. Their urgent kisses made my body melt.

I marked my birthday at the theater. It was a rehearsal night. I tousled my surfer bangs and called to our older friend Crystal Ivey's brother Rick, "Hey, I'm 16!"

Rick pressed a dime into my hand. "Call me when you're 18," he boomed, to make the others laugh. Like Crystal, Rick was in his 30s. He slept in Crystal's pantry with his collection of sci-fi paperbacks. Just the weekend prior, I'd made out with him in the back seat of Crystal's Firebird as she sped down the 110 to San Pedro and home. He'd rubbed my crotch with urgency—an astounding sensation.

Once I saw him shuffling down Pacific Avenue in downtown Pedro, reading as he walked. He looked like any wino near the Longshoreman's Hall. I was alone; I could have greeted him, but I chose not to.

Tonight, we were going someplace special: My Ship, a bigger bar in Manhattan Beach. Crystal told us the front was shaped like an enormous ship's bow. Nidia and I added to our halter dresses white captain's hats she'd found in the costume room.

That night, just around the corner from My Ship, I attended an orgy. Rick brought me. I waited like the proverbial fifth wheel with my captain's hat in my hands while blurry, fleshly things happened around me. I told myself that this was part of the adult life that awaited me, and that choosing to sit this one out was simply a cool, acceptable choice. The hostess was an elementary school teacher. There were stacks of construction paper in the corner of her studio apartment. I regarded the kid art on her fridge.

"How can you leave when you haven't come?" the hostess purred to Rick. Once Rick's pants were up, he walked me back to My Ship. I tried to hold his hand. He squeezed it politely, then released.

Inside, Nidia slumped at a back table, crying. I only spotted her because of that white halter dress. That captain's hat, with its crisp gold braid.

It turned out that Ray, father of four, had rushed to meet Nidia when she arrived at My Ship. His wife had run off in a snit to do coke with her friends. Ray's urgent tongue explored Nidia's ear and switched her on. Then he'd forced her head down and hadn't stopped. And then he'd left her there.

Knowing what I know, would I run them through with steel, those old men? Sure, they were of age, and we were kids. Yes, they were cheating. But now as then, I can use my finger to poke the memory of them and they crumble, as they have, in fact, crumbled. Some are dead. Their girlfriends became their wives who nursed them. In my mind, the men are dust while their girlfriends remain fresh in long vests, flared velvet pants, and watching headbands.

After high school, Nidia and I worked as waitresses in a chain hotel restaurant with an Auld English Theme. The sound of the bar entertainer, a Jerry Lee Lewis impersonator, bled through the adjoining wall. He liked to joke that to him a woman was just life support for a cooter.

Skylab's decaying orbit made it clear: the spent and sickened space shuttle was coming home. NASA hadn't planned well for the shuttle blasting back to earth. No resources were committed to delay its entry or blunt what would occur. That day, Nidia and I spray painted a big target on a white sheet and used it as a picnic blanket at Averill Park.

Nidia and I are both long married and know for ourselves wedlock's charming compromises and suppressed truths. From time to time, we meet up. A different city every visit. We run across town plazas with backpacks bouncing and arms outstretched, calling each other's names.

Peter Frampton is old now, and in failing health. My husband remembers seeing him at Los Angeles's Fabulous Forum back in 1979. By that time, the curly-headed singer's star had already waned. For "I'm in You," Frampton wore a miner's lamp strapped to his angelic head as he probed the audience for love.

THE NEW SPAN

In the back seat, Richard Three works your neck with his tongue and teeth, so smooth he doesn't break his rhythm when night air blasts: you've reached the toll booth. With his free hand, he passes Richard One pre-counted bills, folded lengthwise.

Richard One has extended his arm back for the bill. He smells of fabric softener and onions: he works days at his family's burger shop on Hearst and Shattuck. The crash poles around the toll booth are lumpy with stickers from bands no one ever heard of.

You pass Treasure Island. Richard Two is riding shotgun, with his faded black clothes and dirty hair. There is no music: the car doesn't have a sound system and you all have cheap flip phones.

Three Richards, one next to you in back, his hand down your tights creating magic and his eyes cast out his window, taking in the new span. You're still in your funeral outfit, a plain black sweater and short skirt. Your mom's leopard ballet flats.

The new span is white and modern with white metal slants like harp strings. You glide close to the water. The sky has darkened. On your side, the left, is the metal hulk of the old span, the double-decker one that suffered all that damage in the Loma Prieta earthquake. It's scary in the dark. The gray silhouette of it like a sunken ship, a haunted palace, or a home for horrible fish rising from the Bay mud and making a home in buckled concrete. Where old-time suicides who misjudged leaps battered themselves bloody on its beams.

Richard Two lights and hands Richard One the single hitter. The air inside the car is nicely fuzzy with smoke. The weed had dried your mouth, and you are not sure whether or not you want Richard Three to kiss you.

He speaks. "Did you ever take the F bus from Berkeley and get, like, butterflies seeing the Hills Bros sign and the red words spelling out "Port of"—and then the spire of the Ferry Building and the white clockface—and then "San Francisco"?

"No, I never did that," you answer. You have never seen these lights because you have never headed west to the city at night. The last time you traveled here it was for school clothes with your mother and you weren't speaking. In the middle of the old span, you climbed into the back seat and curled up on the floor behind her. Stiff with anger, you'd stared at the asphalt rushing underneath like a warp-speed river. Wishing her out of your life and yourself, all grown, in an apartment without her.

The three Richards were two years ahead of you at Berkeley High. You knew enough about them to know they would take AC Transit to the TransBay Terminal, then walk to the clubs. You also knew about their band, An Embarrassment of Richards, later shortened to Embarrassment, then simply, Bare Ass. They used to play at parties around town until two of them got girlfriends and the band broke up.

Richard Two, you hate. He says vile things about you behind your back. And, in fact, argued against your being invited tonight. You heard. You also heard Richard Three saying you were okay for a fat girl, that you'd just lost your mother, after all, and had no friends.

It was a stupid fluke they even came to your mom's wake. Richard One has an older sister who rents a room in your apartment. You are roommates now. It's been decided you'll keep that going. The wake was winding down and you were headed to your room when you heard voices inside, and that was the Richards.

Richard Three's fingers have worked some crazy magic and now you are feeling something wholly new, a white light that blurs your vision and makes your body curl to his arm and grasping it, shudder. The Bare Ass laughs, but nicely, and Richard Two tousles your hair. And you see it and you do get butterflies mixed with a kind of fluttery aftereffect of your first orgasm: the red block letter lights spelling out PORT OF and then the Ferry Building with its yellow face and then SAN FRANCISCO.

OVER THE TOWN

When I was a regular adult, I thought nothing would scare me, but I was wrong. Now that I am old, I am afraid all the time.

I visit my beloved at dusk, so early this Boston in November. In the locked ward, patients in floppy slippers walk short laps. We see them pass again and again. A television blares. My beloved's first roommate is a heroin addict, who has been here before and who will leave this ward for somewhere far worse. His second roommate looks like Cary Grant. He left his four children and wife for his male business partner, who then sued and slandered him. This roommate steals my beloved's clothes.

In the common room, I position myself between my beloved and everyone else. Having the others behind me makes my heart beat faster. But my beloved shows no reaction to their voices, the strange and ragged syllables breaking from the mouth of one who is on the hall phone.

When I am with him, I resist the urge to cling. We sit in chairs that are like wide, incredibly heavy recliners that do not tilt back, and stay where they are dragged. They need to be heavy so they cannot be thrown, a nurse explained on your first day.

My beloved is the man of our house, still. This is why I resist returning to my hotel room near the airport with the fluorescent slot of light under the door. Where I caused a flood by overfilling the tub and where I activated the fire alarm microwaving bacon.

Here in Boston, I linger in Places of Historical Interest. The African Meeting House. The Old North Church. The hospital's Maxwell & Eleanor Blum Patient and Family Learning Center, where I can use the printer for my employer's family leave paperwork. Or the hospital gift shop. Or the hospital's massive basement cafeteria, with its thick air and tawdry, New England-accented dramas.

Outside, the weather is harsh and cleansing. I have not brought many clothes from Arizona. Just a leather jacket from DaZee's that I have had for ages and never worn until this trip. I walk through the Boston Common with my metal eyeglasses hurting my face in search of gloves and a hat. I also buy a half-pint of gin. I visit King's Chapel, with boxes for families to sit in instead of pews. After visiting the tiny bathroom for a couple of swallows of gin, I purchase a ticket to the Bell and Bones tour. At the top of a rickety staircase, we are shown an enormous bell, one of the very last crafted by Revere & Sons. In the basement are the crypts, along with boilers, low-hung pipes, and discarded office furniture from the 1970s.

At Mass General, I use the 7th-floor bathroom and finish the gin, sitting on the toilet and scrolling my phone. I set the bottle in the metal sanitary napkin box beside the toilet. On one side of the vault-like doors, I wait to be buzzed in. On the other side, I receive my VISITOR label. I make my way to the nurse's station and wait while the bag of pears and goat cheese I have brought for my beloved is examined. In the common area, I drag two chairs to the wide window that overlooks Boston's North End. I have strength to spare, although I must keep one hand on the glass due to the spins.

When my beloved shuffles out in the maroon hospital shirt and pants, I motion for him to sit beside me. Our tired eyes meet. With a visceral certainty, I know he is taking my strength. But I give this willingly, to help him heal. It is his. It is why I don't sleep, why I spend my food allowance on special treats for him.

Now my beloved motions for me to throw myself with him through the heavy glass window. Together we stand and push through and it's as easy as the ripping split at an aqua hotel pool. We are flying in the keen air, hand in hand. I show him Boston Harbor and the One-if-by-Land-Two-if-by-Sea steeple and the diamond-bright Whole Foods where I get the pears and cheese; the macadamia nuts and dried apricots.

We glide hand-in-hand over the snowy Boston Common. I do not point out the Burying Ground outside of King's Church, with all its brittle-looking and snow-covered headstones, crooked like teeth, and adorned with those sinister Puritan hearts and wings. I do not tell him about the Strangers' Tomb that was part of the Bell and Bones Tour at King's Chapel. How Tomb 21, located directly under the bell tower, holds the remains of 30 to 50 poor souls who came from outside the city and had no money to pay for a burial. The Strangers' Tomb is loaf-shaped and bricked solid. But the guide showed us a picture, and in that picture you could make out a nest of faded red hair.

As if it will keep him safe, I turn my beloved's face to me by the chin, and say, "With this ring, I wee wed," the very words he'd stumbled over at our wedding all those years ago. And we kiss. It is not like those face-abrading kisses of our early days. It is tender. And lingering. And through our oil-on-canvas exchange with its snowy backdrop my husband and I are back home in Tucson. A soft old couple together in matching recliners, a cat for each of our laps.

PARDON ME FOR MOONWALKING

We weren't much more than halfway to Bill and Lila's place at the Russian River when the drugs kicked in. I asked my boyfriend Rocky how he was holding up. "Colorfully," he said, each syllable a separate word. He'd taken the lion's share of the mushrooms. He was also the only one with a driver's license.

My brother Bill and his wife Lila were away for the weekend. Our job was to gather eggs their chickens had laid. Bill had told me fresh blue corn cakes and orange juice awaited us. We should help ourselves to the yellow squash, purple carrots, and heirloom tomatoes in the big raku bowl on the table. These words were talismanic against the littered sidewalk/public transport/soul-sucking day job sameness of our days. The three of us—me, Rocky, and his work friend, Dawn—had jumped at the chance to leave the city. We'd had just enough money for gas, drugs, and a rental car, so long as we refused the insurance.

The psilocybin had leached the moisture from my eyes. I thumbed out my contact lenses. Everything was a smear of light and color. Lounging in the back on a pile of clothes she'd pulled from our bags, Dawn rhapsodized about the sky in her squeaky, babyish voice. "That's pretty, Dawn," Rocky said. "Real pretty." He reached back, gave her bare ankle a squeeze.

At last, we turned into the dark yard. The three of us seeped from the dusty car. The redwood needles gave the ground a springy feeling under my bare feet. The country! That smell! My lungs felt cherished by the night air. Through the windows, yellow light illuminated Lila's huge Hopi sand paintings on either side of the stone hearth. That food was going to taste great.

The spare key was right where Bill had said, under the raccoon statue. The trouble was, it didn't work. We all tried. I worried aloud the key would snap in the lock.

"Bastards!" Rocky growled, jamming his hands into his armpits and hopping from side to side. Any sign of trouble always brought out the New York cabbie he'd been before coming west.

"Guess we break a window," Dawn squeaked. Her eyes were slits. Dawn was always suggesting big moves like this, but she never made anything happen. Mainly she just talked about the 40-Watt Club, back home in Athens, Georgia, and how she'd once partied with the B-52s.

Rocky's olive face was slack. I discerned the vulnerable skull beneath. "Maybe Rue and Angel have a spare," I ventured.

Bill and Lila weren't the only city couple who had moved to the Russian River. Rue and Angel, we knew fairly well. A slight blonde, Angel had once been a boxer. Her ring name was "the Tattooed Angel." Rue was a wild, loud country girl with a gap between her teeth.

We humped back into the rental car. On the passenger side window where I'd stuck them, I spied my withered contact lenses. I popped them into my mouth to soften them up.

Rue and Angel's place was next door to a seedy putt-putt golf course, the one with the giant lavender dinosaur in front. A party was in full swing. A couple of dozen women lounged, danced, or sprawled on the back deck. Inside it was heated up, windows fogged. Hazy warm colors. The Indigo Girls warbled from the speakers. I desperately needed to pee. I barged through the festivities in my department store punk regalia and bare feet.

"If it's yellow, let it mellow," a printed sign above the toilet read. "If it's brown, flush it down. If it's red . . ." I don't remember what you were supposed to do if it was red. I put my contact lenses in my eyes with a minute sucking sound. I knew enough not to look at my reflection.

Back in the living room, Rue spotted me. "Straight girl alert!" she screamed, waving a CD. It was Michael Jackson's Thriller album, old even back then. When I asked about a spare key, she fake-pouted and shook her head.

That was when Angel appeared. She was dressed in a ribbed white undershirt and those Dolphin shorts, ocean blue on one side white on the other. Her slim arms were covered in color. In slow motion, butterflies batted their wings. Snakes undulated. It was one of the most beautiful sights I had ever beheld.

I tried to remind Angel that I was Bill's sister. No words emerged. And then we were dancing, and it was all right, velvety and warm. Angel held her wrists above her head, prettily swiveling her hands. "Smooth Criminal" blared from the speakers.

Then I did it: began moonwalking like Wacko Jacko, bare feet catching on the carpet. Of course, I fell. The music continued, but the conversation did not.

"So, are you okay?" someone said at last.

"Ahyeah! Definitely!" I hollered, heaving myself up. "Pardon me! Pardon!" Away from the Tattooed Angel, away from the dancing, out the door and down the ramp into the cold air.

Rocky and Dawn lounged against the rental car, trying to look casual. Dawn's thumbs were in Rocky's belt loops. I could smell his cologne.

It couldn't have been more clear: they'd just been kissing. I shook my head for more time than made sense. Then I stopped. "Need to go back to the city," I said.

"This is horseshit," Rocky returned darkly.

"We could steal some inner tubes and float the river until daybreak," Dawn offered, not bothering to open her eyes.

Their words hung in the chilling air. A few yards away, Rue and Angel's patio lights swirled. It had been warm inside. It would be so easy to simply return. Moonwalk back—smoothly this time—making it clear my lame moves had been a joke.

I could hear us breathing. Our exhalations visible like those of farm animals. Something felt cool and soothing between my toes. I looked down. I'd stepped on a banana slug.

"You're up." Rocky threw me the rental car keys, so hard they bit.

CLOSING TIME

Fiona banks her ride in front of Mel's Hot & Cold Heroes. Her Oldsmobile Cutlass is like a battered lemon shark. She leaves the motor running, reaches back to smooth the watch plaid blanket across the slippery backseat. The stand's iron grating is drawn against the Cincinnati night. Her man is inside. Mel. Waltzing the mop around. Reeking of grease and onion. His upper arm is inked, Blue Valentine. He doesn't like her to see him dirty. Normally showers and changes before their dates. Buffs his nails. Tonight, she'll get him before the ablutions. Fiona grips the grating. Shakes it.

IT IS THE SUMMER OF SKYLAB

Skylab has orbited Earth for a long time. In the end, its decaying orbit makes it clear: the spent and sickened space shuttle is coming home.

The news is filled with speculation as to where the U.S.'s first space station will plunge back to Earth. Kyle and Cheri joke that they should pack a lunch, spray paint a big target on a white sheet and use it as a picnic blanket.

Instead, they do what they always do. Wait for his folks to leave for swing shift at Todd Shipyard and fuck in Kyle's boyhood room.

"You should have been here last night," Kyle says afterward. "My mom outdid herself. She and Chuck were blotto. She started in on how no one appreciates her; how we don't care if she lives or dies. For the grand finale, she lifted her nightgown and peed on the living room floor."

"Jesus Christ!" But Cheri's reaction is perfunctory. She's become used to such stories. "Oh, I'm on my period; forgot to tell you."

"Here." Kyle dips for his t-shirt. Automatically, Cheri throws an arm across him so he doesn't fall. He stuffs his shirt under her rear. Will they ever again be so careless with the sharing of their bodies? The carnal fluids, the nicknames for genitals. They'd learned on each other. Mainly in Kyle's car, a huge gray beater he likes to call the land shark.

"I gotta pee. Then I'm making popcorn." Naked, Kyle rolls out of the bed. Hits the floor with a little jump. His belly jiggles.

Cheri knows Kyle's sci-fi books and World War II maps by heart. Has dozed clutching the now-eyeless teddy bear Kyle's father, Big Kyle, left him when he took off. Kyle is a year older than Cheri. So it's been his prom, then hers. His graduation. Hers. They have recently been fired from Anthony's Pizza Paradise, for advising the owner that the minimum wage has gone up ten cents an hour. Later today there is an interview at the 99-cent Theater on Crenshaw and PCH. They saw Rocky II last night, to check the place out. If they land the gig, they'll pretend they are only friends.

Cheri spies a paperback-sized volume on his desk, green with a blank spine. Kyle keeps a diary? Idly, she opens it. A list of couples: Kyle's name is paired with Janice, Cheri's best friend since second grade. Cheri's is matched with a name she doesn't even recognize. She knows Kyle well enough to piece together it's his post-apocalyptic wish list. A few supplies are listed as needed for the new community of eight to "FLOURISH."

She thumbs back to last April when she and Kyle lost their virginity together. It had actually been sort of lovely and romantic. Kyle had a buddy who worked at the Knight's Retreat in Lomita. He'd set them up in a vacant room, very clean, left a pile of vending machine goodies on the dresser.

"A 'cherry' time," is scrawled in Kyle's green book. That's it. Just a smirky note in the top corner. The main entry covers a chemistry exam, and an upcoming wrestling match.

"Yoo-hoo!" Kyle elbows the door ajar, holding the bowl of popcorn in one hand. With the other, he dangles her used tampon. In their hurry for bed, she'd left it on the corner of the tub.

Cheri and Kyle are compatible in an extremely basic way that they allow to fill every minute of their time. Cheri understands this. Knows that her oft-uttered wish to attend college in Northampton, Massachusetts will never become manifest. She has gotten as far as marking flecked cardigans and corduroy dirndls in the Sears catalog, but in fact has applied to no college anywhere.

NASA hasn't planned for the shuttle's return, or where all those pieces would scatter. There have been zero resources committed to delaying its reentry, or neutralizing it to float around forever as space junk, or blunting what was about to happen somewhere on Earth.

The chances are slim that Skylab will land in the Rancho San Pedro housing project near the Port of Los Angeles. But it could happen. Skylab, emerging from the misty smog to find Kyle and Cheri.

She thought of Kyle's vision. Certainly, they would remain unscathed. The world around them might be torched black. But she and Kyle and their ready cohort in the Rancho San Pedro housing project—well, they had provisions.

COOL GRAY PALE BLUE SILVER

I first knew Seth as a towheaded four-year-old, sticky fingers entwined in my hair. Every couple of weeks, he and his hippie father and sisters would hitch to San Francisco from Humboldt. They were delivering weed to my dealer friends, Dwight and Gregg.

I worked part-time for a movie distributor. Part of my job in this analog time involved phoning movie theaters late at night, after they'd sold tickets to their last shows. I had no phone. I wanted quiet to focus on my painting. At the appointed hour, I'd take my muslin bag of quarters to the corner pay phone. Then I thumbed the coins into the slot and jotted down the ticket sales for Outrageous Fortune or Tin Men.

Dwight and Gregg, my weed dealers, were my only friends. Our apartments were close to the Hyde Street cable car line. Dwight saved my life by grabbing the back of my jacket as I was about to step into the Hyde car's path one day.

I soon learned that everyone was furious at Dwight for swallowing a fistful of pills when Gregg had only taken little Seth to Cala Foods. As for Gregg, he was always in hot water for disappearing for days at a time with a new crush.

In the new year, I'd sometimes ring their doorbell and be told by Gregg they were in bed with achy muscles, headaches. That cleared up, but then they both fell more seriously ill.

I understood little about AIDS in those days. Later, I would know many without means who endured the tortures wrought by the new drug, AZT, and then complications from AIDS itself.

Seth, his hippie father, and two sisters moved in. They took care of Dwight and Gregg. The girls cooked and cleaned. Little Seth and his father entertained friends who came to visit, including me.

One watery afternoon, Dwight told me about the experimental drug he and Gregg had been given at SF General. AZT was the great hope—indeed the only hope—for those who had contracted HIV. He spoke with effort, sitting in his club chair as in the old days, but his thin shoulders were covered with a blanket. One side effect was images of horrific violence every time he closed his eyes, he told me. For Gregg, head and muscle aches made his waking hours hard to bear.

"Seth knows I can't enforce any rules, Dwight said. "He could so easily go off the rails."

But to me, at the fringes of their life and grappling with problems of my own, Seth stayed the same. He turned five. At Dwight's insistence, he started kindergarten in the neighborhood. He loved his little classmates, his cubby, and his teacher. Every day after school, he would skip down the hill to where I waited for him.

When I arrived for one visit, Dwight and Gregg were both resting. Between them, Seth napped. One of the girls brought me a Bloody Mary and a little plate of saltines with goat cheese and rosemary.

I began planning a weekend trip back home to Los Angeles. I aimed to reconnect with my parents and ask them for a loan. On impulse, I asked Seth's dad if I could take Seth to Disneyland. To his credit, he hesitated before saying yes.

Recently, one of Dwight and Gregg's friends had died in Seth's arms at SF General. His pale sisters didn't even attend school.

Seth's father leaned forward to hold my gaze. I understood that this was his way of signaling his assessment of my ability to care for his son. Or at least appearing to do so.

It would just be for the weekend, I said. And the following week was Spring Break at Seth's school.

For an instant, his father looked surprised at this news, before his face settled back into calm, and he said it was a good idea. He smelled of patchouli, a new scent to me back then.

This smell spoke to me of open skies and faraway places. Nothing like my life of painting and getting high and dodging my landlord.

Then he kissed me. It was unlike the hard pressings and wet urgency of the high school boys I'd known. He was unhurried. Even passive, poking his tongue between my lips but then not moving it. One of his daughters came in to say she needed to order more checks. Her hair was puffed up in a tangle in the crown, like a small child's.

I have a photo of me and Seth from our trip, in line for the Haunted Mansion. A red-haired mom with tattooed arms—an unusual thing back then—offered to take it with her disposable camera and mail it to me.

After the photo was snapped, Seth asked me to raise him. I pretended he was joking. "We could be a little family," he said, looking up at me with his brown, turned-down-at-the-corners eyes. What else could I do? I was 19 years old, spending money I didn't have on weed and cocaine, barely able to make rent. I wrapped my arms around Seth and inhaled the smell of his hair, his unlaundered clothes. In better days, Dwight and I had talked about me taking over their weed business. But nothing had transpired, and we both knew I was neither friendly nor detail-oriented enough to make a go of it.

Spring Break came. My parents hadn't come through on the loan, as I had hoped. I came home to a pale blue eviction notice taped to my apartment door. The next Monday, I stood at the bottom on California Street at noon as usual. I'd received the photograph of us at Disneyland and couldn't wait to give it to Seth. In the photo, we are both wearing jean jackets and yellow Captain EO sunglasses.

But there was no sign of Seth and his characteristic skip. Chinese grandmothers shuffled past with their kindergartners. I went to Dwight and Gregg's flat and rang the buzzer. No one came. The same thing happened the next day, and the next.

I tried again late at night. The street was so quiet I could hear the buzzer sounding in the empty apartment. I pictured Seth with his father and sisters, shivering on the side of the road in the dark for a ride to Humboldt. And what about Dwight and Gregg? It sounds crazy for them to have been jailed for dealing, or to have moved away, sick as they were. But in the late 1980s in San Francisco, when I was in my early twenties, people vanishing or suddenly moving across the country, or dying began to occur with increasing frequency. This story takes place at a time when I was increasingly lost myself, and not nearly as good a friend to people in need as I would be if it were now, so many years later.

It was time to make my calls from the corner pay phone. Down the hill, the lights of the financial district glittered through the mist. I made the calls with the photo of me and Seth propped before me in the booth. When I was done, I replaced the hard plastic receiver in its cradle. A few coins dropped to the coin return, and I tucked them into my fabric bag. But the coins kept coming. Faster and faster, it seemed. I could no longer catch them all. What in the hell had I done to deserve such a break? "Nothing." Breath coming fast in the white-lit booth, I watched the coins wheel and skitter at my feet.

MAN ON THE MOON

My mother and I nurse small wounds on our fingers. We're sweating at her kitchen table making daisies out of can lids she's saved all month. On the black and white television we've moved to a kitchen chair, history unfolds in space. Apollo 11. Nine years have passed since President Kennedy intoned to a special joint session of Congress: *"I believe this nation should commit itself to achieving the goal, before this decade is out, of landing a man on the moon and returning him safely to Earth."*

We use a special pair of snippers to cut the metal. The white and yellow paint I found in my mother's tiny garage. We talk about coupons and curlers and reducing diets. One of her eyes is made up with liner and sky-blue shadow; the other is naked and tired.

My brother would use can lids as ineffective ashtrays. Ashes still cling to the fibers of the carpet under his window. He'd sit on the sill to watch the stars. He knew all about the cosmos. He was saving for first and last on an apartment in Cocoa. He'd have a view of Cape Canaveral from his balcony. A front-row seat to roaring black space.

The last time I saw him, he was crawling on the floor, eyes wild, begging me to draw the curtains. He clung to my legs and asked if he could sleep on my floor. I didn't answer him. *I didn't answer.* As if his sputtering light, the sounds he made, died before reaching me.

I slice my thumb and gasp. On my mother's kitchen chair,
Neil Armstrong sets foot on the lunar surface.

LOOSIES

In the daytime, the air was filled with the smell of the nearby refinery and the discount bakery where Daphne worked. The crack of the bats from the little league field.

Nights were different. It was the year Daphne's guy classmates became her lovers. At least that was how Daphne framed it to herself. They would come to her late at night, after frustrating sessions with their girlfriends. She collected and kept their semen in squares of aluminum foil, which she stored in the nightstand beside her twin bed. The yellow-lit air was punctuated by the sound of foghorns and the freight train's moan.

After graduation, her English teacher, Mr. Clark, invited her to live with him in swanky Santa Monica. Mr. Clark was an apple-cheeked Midwesterner with a nice car, and belts with tasteful silver buckles. A rack of pastel-colored neckties. He called himself a movie buff. In his rent-controlled apartment, he had an entire armoire fitted out with shelves for his movies. His kitchen cupboards were stocked with Fiesta ware dishes and fancy jam. Daphne awoke each day to beach haze and the swish of palms outside the bedroom window. Slim joggers like a string of rosary beads traversing Montana Avenue. It felt like a different world from the blue-collar town where she'd grown up. Mr. Clark's decency was a brand-new page atop her blurry, messy senior year. She'd barely passed her classes.

For Daphne, sex was like a needed scouring. Searing her the way cold soda burns the back of the throat. But Mr. Clark was tender. Sometimes he talked about his day teaching as he undressed. Sex with him always began lying down. It included a lot of eye contact.

Mr. Clark introduced her to his friend, Matteo. Matteo lived just down the street, close to the Montana Avenue branch of the Santa Monica library. The floors of his bachelor pad were bare wood, and a red drum kit was set up in the middle of the living room. Matteo shaved his hair close, like a shadow against his dark skin. His legs were muscled and nearly hairless; he gleamed. Matteo was the only person Daphne had ever met who grew up in Malibu.

Sitting at a cafe, Matteo told them about his French ex-girlfriend, who had said as she was breaking up that she was available to him for sex at any time. She adored their skins together, she had told him so in her marvelous voice.

Back at his apartment, Mr. Clark told Daphne about sitting under the table when his mother had her bridge club friends over. He'd get aroused at the sight of their legs, he said. Years later, he'd even had an affair with one of them. Just like The Last Picture Show, he added. Mr. Clark told her this at the dinner table, shirtless. Maybe he was trying to add a little frisson of worldliness, like Matteo with his French ex-girlfriend. But Mr. Clark was pale, with a hairy nascent paunch and pink nipples that made Daphne avert her gaze.

Daphne began struggling with insomnia. At work, she'd doze at her desk. One night, when Mr. Clark was at an evening meeting at the school, she called Matteo to ask if he had anything she could take. The intimacy of his voice in her ear gave her a feeling like the door to a little birdcage in her chest was floating open. He guessed they could meet at the Thai restaurant on Wilshire, he said after a pause. She got the message: they shouldn't meet at either apartment, even though both were closer than the restaurant.

Once there, Matteo kept it buddy-buddy. He ordered tea without food, then handed her a single capsule over her plate of *pad see-ew*. Under the bright lights, she saw a wariness there. Or was it concern for her?

The next day, a Simi Valley jury acquitted four Los Angeles Police Department officers of assault. Three were also acquitted of excessive force against a construction worker named Rodney King. But Daphne had seen the brutality in the video footage taken from an overlooking apartment window. Everybody had seen it.

When the story broke, she was in her cubicle listening to KCRW. The elderly CEO messaged from his home office in faraway Calabasas that everyone had better go home. Make sure to stock up on water, he added.

Unlike the town where Daphne grew up, her workplace and apartment were miles from the uprising the news reported. It took two hours to drive the three miles to Santa Monica. At the convenience store, the water shelf was bare, so she got packages of dried ramen noodles and candy. Everyone in line was white. No one looked at each other or spoke. It was the kind of place that sold plastic lighters and "loosies," or loose cigarettes of indeterminate make. She added four and smoked one in her car.

Mr. Clark and Matteo and Daphne spent the evening together on the couch, eating the candy. Instead of the news, they watched To Sir, With Love. Matteo and Mr. Clark drank the beers Matteo had brought. Daphne sat in the middle holding both of their hands.

Mr. Clark and Matteo argued playfully about who was "Sir," the teacher played by Sidney Poitier in the movie. "If you want to dance wif me, you bleedin' well ask proper!" Daphne squeaked like the girl in the movie. Matteo put his sweater across her legs and Mr. Clark patted her knee.

The movie ended. The candy was almost gone. The three stood in the doorway in silence, blowing smoke from their loosies into the night. The smoke drifted back to them and into the apartment. It didn't matter, Daphne said. Finally, Matteo said he guessed he'd better hit it. He and Mr. Clark shook hands, an oddly formal gesture.

Daphne found herself seized with an animal need for Matteo to stay, rather than travel the two blocks home. This feeling was not sexual, as Mr. Clark would have thought had Daphne released the cry trapped in her throat.

She watched Matteo walk up 19th Avenue for as long as she could see him in the silent, yellow-lit street. The stars in the sky were like cold and faraway fires. She remembered something Matteo had told her at the Thai restaurant, when she couldn't sleep and he'd handed her one of his sleeping pills. He had said that even the meager strands that bound him to his life—he was single, didn't own a home, had no children—seemed at times too heavy.

"What do you want?" she'd asked. She wasn't flirting or hoping for physical intimacy although she probably wouldn't have turned him down had he asked.

"I want to be a molecule. In a piece of toast, say," he'd answered. "Doing a job. Regarded by no one."

Now Daphne bent for the cigarette ends they'd dropped and Matteo had extinguished with the tip of his shoe. The birdcage door in her chest stirred and she started to cry. Drunk on three beers, Clark lobbed miniature candy bars at her back.

WE ARE ALL SITTING DOWN TO MIRACLE MONDAY

Everyone's brought leftovers from Christmas. Sasha says the miracle will be if no one dies from food poisoning. But it's the first day everyone could make it. And the miracle is that we all survived the holidays with our families.

I am in a foul mood. I meant to get spiffed up, but I stopped halfway. So, I'm in a pencil skirt and too-small t-shirt with a faded picture of Betty Boop on the tit. Period cramps: terrible. Makeup: half-assed.

My girlfriend Sasha has been fired from her temp job for pressing her boobs against a glass conference room wall, 26 floors up. Our heater is broken, and so is our oven. Luckily our next-door neighbor seems to be out, and I still have her key from when we watched her place last summer. So her oven is ours.

Brian and his young boyfriend Frankie worked a brunch in Golden Gate Park, and arrive bearing two shrimp trees, a jar of cocktail sauce, and a double magnum of bubbly they've stolen. Brian calls their black pants and white shirts their "retail drag." Their closet at home is stuffed with items they've liberated from Macy's.

Larry brings his Ukrainian workmate Pat, who we all like to have around because he is the only real punk we know. It's only a matter of time before Pat gets blackout drunk and throws a punch. It's happened every single time I've seen him. On Halloween, he and Brian ended up on the sidewalk, snarling in their clown costumes. But I know Pat spent Christmas alone. He kisses my cheek, and I hear the swish of chains on his leather jacket. He really is so gentlemanly at the beginning of things.

Larry is wolfing down shrimp, dragging them through the plate of ketchuppy sauce. One of the shrimp trees is nearly defenestrated. He is keeping an eye on Pat, who is telling how he awoke on the sand on Ocean Beach without his wallet and glasses.

We are six, then. Displayed before us are five bowls of cranberry sauce. A pile of turkey skin on a plate. The rolls and bowl of mashed potatoes are down the hall in my neighbor's oven. We pass around a joint. I pass around spoons and soon the cranberry is making its way around. Brian refills our glasses from the magnum of warm bubbly. The tablecloth is soaked with it.

Frankie offers to check the oven down the hall. Our dog, Ruby, snuffles around our feet. I keep handing down bits of turkey skin. She licks my hand. We don't have fairy lights, but the streetlight streaming in illuminates the raindrops on the windows. It is a moment to behold.

Everybody starts saying what they are thankful for. My feet in their socks are nicely warm, then I realize Ruby has thrown up on them. That's when Frankie bursts in. There's a fire next door in the neighbor's kitchen. He couldn't control it. He's dramatically backlit by gray smoke, like a performer on stage. Then I realize he is crying. He thinks he's in trouble. We are all so young, but Frankie is even younger.

Beside me, Pat lurches to his feet like a skinny bear, a growl beginning in his chest.

BUCKETS

Randy and Taiko are standing at the chimp habitat. Taiko doesn't recall the sight of the chimps ever affecting her this way. They just look so miserable. One perches atop a fat jutting pole. Rounded like driftwood. Do apes heave sighs? This one looks about to.

Taiko and Randy are the things that don't belong. The zoo is a small but nice one. Less than a mile from their modest home. This is their first visit in years. They are neither the age of the unshowered mothers and tousle-headed fathers, nor the grandparents with their utility hairstyles and dark blue jeans.

They watch—along with the melancholy chimp—as a young mom, no makeup, hair scraped back, tucks Cheerios into her toddler's upturned mouth. "Go with Daddy," says the mom when she is done.

A gaggle of four-year-olds arrives, herded by their teacher and an elderly male docent. They stand against the glass, watching the chimp with solemn eyes. The docent is explaining that when human beings make eye contact, it means we are curious. "It means something different to these guys," he says.

"What about smiling?" a fat little boy asks.

"Well, to them it might mean you're angry," the old man says. As if in response, the chimp circumnavigates the enclosure, swinging and screaming. When he drops to the ground, the docent tells the children to get back. Their damp handprints vanish from the glass.

On the way to the brand-new sky ride, they pass the old retired one, the one they used to ride with their kids. The mechanism remains, its pale-yellow buckets stilled. How nervous it had made Taiko to ascend in the old ride, just a few yards above the slumbering tiger.

In contrast, the new "aerial gondolas" are carpeted and enclosed. One by one, they glide to an almost stop on a wide concrete pad. Plenty of young staff members are there to guide riders in. Taiko and Randy sit across from each other.

It is only when they're alone that he reassures her that he intends to stay connected. He'll be living with his girlfriend at her apartment. Taiko will keep the house. They'll tell the kids later, on Skype. Neither of them has slept.

Taiko says at last, "This place is a kind of portal." To their earlier years, she means. Imparting the animals' habitats, eating preferences, and extinction statuses as though they weren't reading from the placards. The Cheerios, the umbrella strollers; all of it. They pass a large billboard, announcing the future home of brown bears, buffalo, and eagles. California fauna. "This was a bad idea," she says.

Back on terra firma, Randy excuses himself to use the restroom. He asks if she'll be okay, and Taiko snaps, "Of course." She regards the hyenas. She doesn't recall them looking so sinister. A young mom in yoga pants approaches with her kids: a toddler boy and an older girl. The children begin laughing, loudly and falsely. Taiko realizes why: they are called "laughing" hyenas. She tries to join in, but her laugh comes out more like a bark, or sob. The mom and the girl look alarmed, but the son shambles over to Taiko and takes her face in his sticky hands. He meets her eyes and smiles at her with tiny wet teeth.

EVERYTHING IS ABOUT TO GO WRONG, BUT SO FAR IT HASN'T

Now that high school was over, Kyle and Cheri were ready to move in together.

Cheri's friend who had moved to New York City after graduation sent Kyle and Cheri a poster: Rousseau's The Sleeping Gypsy. In high school, there had been a trip to New York and the Museum of Modern Art. The Sleeping Gypsy depicted a slumbering mandolin player, her instrument and water jar beside her. A lion stood beside her in peace. In New York City, when their love was new, Kyle and Cheri had argued playfully about whether the lion had chosen to leave the gypsy in slumber or simply hadn't devoured her yet.

They bought a couch so lightweight Kyle could pick it up himself. Cheri's grandmother gave them an old refrigerator that made Cheri think of The Maltese Falcon. Several mornings a month, they'd find little mounds of jewel-like windshield glass in the gutter. But so far, Kyle's car had been safe.

One morning the landlord knocked on their door to ask if they'd heard any sounds in the night. Their next-door neighbor had been robbed. He was an elderly man who played the banjo late at night. While Cheri and Kyle lay together in Kyle's childhood bed, they would listen. The old man played songs they didn't recognize, but which summoned sensual nights in Sevierville, Tennessee, where he came from. But they hadn't registered the disturbance.

Cheri spent the evening reading and drinking diet root beer on the flimsy couch, while Kyle surveyed his World War II maps and masturbated sulkily in the second bedroom.

Now it was late. The old man began playing his banjo, his aloneness seeping from the instrument like tea into water. The teenaged lovers lay there side by side, listening. It was so quiet they could hear their neighbor's fingers as they touched the strings.

OXYGEN

Gina and Nadine sat in the cool sand of RAT beach. As planned, Nadine brought along a thermos of diet ginger ale. Gina brought her father's scotch in a bota bag, kidney-shaped in a Navajo print. The girls had mixed them up in the jeep.

They wore their swimsuits beneath their clothes. It was too early for the beach, but Nadine's brother and his friend Chris Gonzalez were surfers.

In her brother's jeep on the way over, Nadine asked Gina loudly whether she'd gotten her period. Gina said no. Nadine said Gina was lucky. She didn't have to worry about getting pregnant. Then she called out to Chris Gonzalez in front that it was Gina's 15th birthday and prodded, "Isn't she hot? Doesn't she look older?"

"Too much bounce to the ounce," he answered lightly. Nadine cried,

"Be nice to my charity case!" She gave Chris Gonzalez a playful shove.

Gina only knew Nadine from a distance, even though the two girls were next-door neighbors. Nadine was older, sixteen. Her mother worked, had frosted hair and French tips.

Last night, Gina was curled on her dining room floor, weeping to Rock and Roll Suicide and feeling that David Bowie and only David Bowie would ever understand her. Then the phone rang, and then her dad was looking down on Gina with his sad eyes. It was Nadine from next door. Did Gina want to go to the beach? Gina's father acted as though Gina got invitations to activities all the time.

"Go," her father urged. "Get out of the house. Some fresh air."

Gina's dad was a butcher. A union man, so the family had great insurance. Gina had sort of known that, but it sounded different coming from Nadine on the way to the beach. She must have heard it from her mother.

Two blond guys traversed the sand in candy-colored Speedos and rubber sandals with socks. They chattered in another language and showed white teeth. German, maybe. They set their ice chest down closest to Gina and lowered themselves to the sand. One pulled out a can of Heineken. The guy beside Gina reclined on his back. As discreetly as she was able, she watched. That's when she saw it: the tent in front of his bathing suit. A straight-up boner as though in salute. A salute to Gina. He grinned at the sky.

Heart pounding, she ducked. Peered again. He took his time turning onto his front. A fullness bloomed in her lower belly.

"We are totally, like, merrrmaids," Nadine was saying. She slowly pulled her sundress over her head. "Drunk mermaids!" she cried, wiping her eyes with the back of her hands. Her bikini was crocheted, the same parrot green as her brother's Jeep. Gina's—which Nadine's mother loaned her, saying it was Nadine's from last year—was strapless and nylon. The top barely covered her.

Nadine turned to Gina. "C'mon, air them titties out." Her voice was in that higher register she used back in the jeep.

"I call this the wonder spot," Nadine continues. She smeared her shoulders with Hawaiian Tropic. It smelled good, like cookies. "Because when I sit here, wonderful guys appear!" She cut her eyes to the two blonds.

Nadine lay down on her front; reached back to unfasten her top. Gina took her time doing the same. Slowly she turned and opened her eyes. Her guy was looking directly at her. This time, Gina stared until he turned away.

One of the reasons Gina stayed inside was that her mother never learned to drive. She broke all the rules of how to be a Southern California mom. Inside, Gina and her mom and sisters read. Tried new recipes. Watch the Million Dollar Movie. Their mom, in full makeup and a hostess gown, pronounces them all "indoorsy."

Everything was okay as long as they all stayed inside.

The sunlight breaks through the clouds. Gina was no mermaid. Just a wobble-legged mammal unaccustomed to the sun. Still, she was at RAT Beach with a popular almost-16-year-old. Most importantly, a college man had chosen Gina to reveal his most intimate physical feeling to.

Back in the Jeep, Nadine gave Gina a head's up that on the way home from the beach, Chris Gonzalez would ride in the back with her if he wasn't too tired from surfing.

"Isn't it weird how they call this beach Rats?" Nadine asked in her normal voice. Her breath was rank. Her glance slid over the lifeguard station, and Gina realized: she thought it was because rats were here.

Gina rose. "It's an acronym," she says. "Right After Torrance. Get it?" She gazed at the water and held for a beat.

"Oh my god," Nadine breathed.

Gina gave a fake-surprised chirp and dipped slowly for the bathing suit top. She took her time situating the front, then inclined her head for Nadine to tie the back. The older girl obeyed.

The warmth of the sand felt good under her feet. Unclotted and pure. From the corner of her eye, she saw the

European boys rise. These college men from halfway around the world were about to follow them into the sea.

Gina would enter the water with Nadine close behind. And then Nadine would grab Gina's wrist. Mutter that Gina was bleeding; that she thought Gina hadn't yet gotten her period; that Gina ruined her bathing suit and would need to pay.

With the worldliness and manners of older men—the college boys would take off jogging down the beach as though that had always been their plan.

And the two girls would see on the surfer's side, Nadine's brother and Chris Gonzalez, sleek dark heads in the water, waiting for their waves. And Nadine would say with her mouth in a line, get in and wash off or else, and Nadine would also say sharks.

And the seawater would sigh, "Ah. Ah. Ah." Each timeless wavelet releasing its oxygen.

TIES THAT BIND

Ricardo is fiddling with the syrups—the same array IHOP has on every table—and staring at my ribbons. We are both 16. I'm wearing a white peasant top with a slit in the front and two white ribbons to tie or not.

Everyone knows Ricardo is in love with me, including his girlfriend, who is a year older, and my mechanic boyfriend, who doesn't consider frail Ricardo a threat. Ricardo fell in love years ago, watching me jog around the middle school track; around and around. He had a doctor's note and never participated in gym class.

We talked for months about meeting for breakfast before school one day during senior year. Now, from this IHOP halfway between home and school, we each pay our share for our pancakes and eggs, then head not to second period but to Richard's house.

I know Ricardo's mother slightly because she works in the office of the elementary school. His father, a twinkle-eyed leading man on the community theater scene, lives in a tiki-themed apartment building in Torrance.

I have no real plan to be unfaithful to my mechanic boyfriend. Plus, I am pretty sure Ricardo is a virgin like me. My boyfriend and I do everything else in the front seat of his gigantic old car, which smells like grease and dust. But there is Richard's older girlfriend to consider. Perhaps he has gained sexual experience and possesses knowledge I have no idea about.

For all I know, his father's apartment is a veritable playground for lovers.

Sitting beside me on his mother's bed, Ricardo leans in for a kiss. His mouth is open but his tongue stays back. I think of a moray eel in its hole, watching and waiting. Then Ricardo bends farther, but rather than making a move, he reaches past me to the nightstand drawer. Lifts something out. It is a small leathery apparatus with a red ball in the middle. It looks like a cat toy.

"Know what this is?" he asks.

"Not really," I say.

That's when he opens his hand to show me a Polaroid picture of his mother, Mrs. Cassidy, with that red hair, that gap between her front teeth. The ball gag secured around her head with her eyes, animal wild.

Ricardo gives a knowing half-smile. The wings of his nostrils are pink and his breath has quickened. He ties my blouse's white ribbons in a bow. Then he knots the loops, pulling tight.

THE LITTLE JENNY

Back in San Francisco, I'd press up behind Van on his Harley, curving up and down Market Street and the Portola. When he'd told me it was over, I bawled his name into the night air. To stop making a goddamn fool of myself, I soon accepted a blind date with a doctor's son who lived in Los Angeles.

Van tracked me there. I agreed to meet him at an Italian place in Los Feliz. My fiancée was spending the summer in Wyoming, where he'd grown up. It was one of my favorite things about him. He wore cowboy boots and owned a truck. I was due to meet him in Jackson Hole in a week.

After an awkward dinner, we took Van's bulldog—Teddy didn't remember me, but we pretended he did—for a stroll. Van had the same slightly bowlegged walk, a weight trainer's gait. The same muscular forearms. Before we reached my car, Van confessed it: he'd moved to L.A. to claim me. He stroked my arm—something he'd never done back in San Francisco when my very cells would yearn for his skin. They remembered him, all right.

We stood with mist falling and water singing in the gutters. A sound—not quite a growl—started in his throat. I knew this sound. My skin and every secret spot knew it. Now he pressed me hard against my car. Our bodies fit. Our mouths opened. It was as though he'd never dropped me in front of my apartment, never ignored my cry as he rounded the corner.

His bed smelled exactly as I remembered, like ink and green onions. I'd worn my everyday bra and underpants, now on the floor in a tumble. Van tipped my pelvis like an urn. Tasted. When he fully took possession of me, I buried my cry in a pillow.

Still, when Van cooked me eggs and suggested we elope, I laughed. The next day I left for Wyoming.

My fiancé's family called the tiny second cabin the Doll House. They'd never put in any water or graveled the drive. The Doll House had no steps to the front door. I'd stand on an overturned plastic bucket and hop in. Inside was my sleeping bag, the giant wooden spool where I'd set up my laptop, and the kitchen chair I'd dragged from the main cabin. The air was thick with the scent of sun-heated wood.

When I wanted to smoke or amble along the cow path lined with quaking aspen, I'd jump back out. The cows regarded me with their wet eyes. We'd breathe together.

The peach body spray I'd bought at the airport mixed with sage and fertile dirt, the stink of manure from the spread next door. Across Highway 189 sat the massive Little Jenny Ranch. Beyond that, the Gros Ventre Wilderness.

It was a special interlude we had going. Sunlight sex on one or the other of the 70s-era daybeds. For breakfast, the Branding Iron Café, and once, the raucous Elkhorn Bar. There was also a tiny post office. A library made of logs held racks of paperbacks with pink spines embracing lovers on every cover.

At dusk, we'd cross the highway and walk at the Little Jenny Ranch, where herds of elk, moose, Rocky Mountain bighorn sheep, and mule deer roamed.

We were sitting before the wide front window. We'd just finished our pot pies and cans of beer. The next day, we planned to drive to Jackson and hike at Jenny Lake, in Grand Teton National Park. We'd postponed twice already, due to rain.

"It's safe here—right?" he said, leaning back in his chair. His gold hair shone.

I rose and laid my head against his chest. But I'd registered the lines under his eyes. Their recession. He was cycling to a blue mood, to a place where even his medication would not help.

He asked if I minded sleeping in the Doll House. Just a little alone time, he said. He asked for this sometimes back in L.A.. I'd really thought in this peaceful place, away from the stresses and worries of home, he'd gotten stronger.

"Jenny Lake will wait," I said. He visibly relaxed.

He planned to stay in Wyoming for a few more months. I needed to get back to L.A. to work. Then we'd see. No way was I calling Van. I saw myself sleeping in a bed filled with books, becoming a regular at the women's bookstore in town. We would see. I made my way to the Doll House, climbed inside, and slipped into my sleeping bag.

Hours later, I awoke and stood in the Doll House doorway. In that sea of sky, the stars stood sharp and clean. In the main cabin, I saw my man with his book. His lugubrious mien, his gold hair illuminated like a Russian icon under the lamp's yellow light.

Despite my inability to make him a happy person, my Wyoming man and I had been good together. We still were. I knew my love for him couldn't make him whole. He'd continue to rely on his parents for money. I'd always work. After the summer, he'd sit in his camping chair in front of our bungalow, long legs stretched out, telling me again about the tiger documentary he'd make someday. His blue moods would swell and fill more of our lives. That wasn't what pushed me to leave. It was what bound me to him. But I wouldn't, couldn't keep hurting him.

On the highway outside, trucks rumbled past. Some were headed northeast toward Jackson Hole. Others, southwest to hardscrabble Pinedale ("All the Civilization You Need") or farther to Rock Springs, once the murder capital of the nation.

My Wyoming man had grown up in those rough environs. His father was the town doctor, who bought his sensitive son a Shetland pony. It was hush-hush; the wildcatters' sons couldn't know. They treated him too roughly as it was.

YOUR HOME TOWN

During pregnancy, cells from the fetus cross the placenta and enter the mother's body, where they can become part of her tissues.

Rounded hills overlook the low town that birthed you. Daytime is the crack of little league bats. The Wednesday "fish wrapper" delivered by a towheaded neighbor. The discount bakery and the smell of hot white bread. Your father works long hours as a butcher. From the bedroom window, you and your sisters can see the green-blue Vincent Thomas Bridge, leading to the Terminal Island canneries and the women's prison. Your aunt leaves her spinster's studio to supervise you girls while your mother does her time.

This cellular invasion means that mothers carry unique genetic material from their children's bodies, creating what biologists call a microchimera, named for a monster from Greek mythology that was part lion, goat, and dragon.

Eastward squat the pumpkinlike tanks of the Los Angeles refinery. At night, its spires are magic: emitting dragon breath plumes. The scene is gold-lit at night.

A whale skeleton is discovered embedded within the refinery grounds. Dubbed Raquel, because her bones are "well-stacked." Your aunt drags you sisters to the excavation site. She sells cans of Bubble Up and Dr Pepper from a folding chair, exchanging raunchy jokes with the diggers and their assistants. You and your sisters climb spiraling metal stairs with boys from Wilmington and Harbor City. Your mother stays gone.

Chimera: a fire-breathing monster, which, according to the Homeric poems, was of divine origin. She was brought up by Amisodarus, king of Caria, and afterward made great havoc in all the country around and among men.

In the night's soul womb, foghorns and the train spread their sonic balm. You sisters have scattered across the land. Been loved by a hundred men. Part of you remains, embedded in the town's tissue, adrift in its petroleum perfume.

HUSBANDRY

My landlord has left a lumpily-rolled joint on my breakfast bar. "Doo-be mellow!" his note says. I don't really mind that he keeps barging in. A lean and sporty retiree, he pities me because I have no furniture. Every day I return to something new: a couch, a chair, a king-sized bed.

Here in the Central Valley the air is sweltering, redolent with grasses and fecund wine grapes, cow piss baked into dirt. My new life as a graduate student.

With all that happened between my ex and me, I arrived too late to find an apartment near the university. I broadened my search to the Capitol, thirteen miles west on eye-80 from my school. My bed is filled with the books I'd packed into the back of my car when I left L.A.. Classes start in two days.

In other words, I am doing okay until my ex-husband finds me.

The day I return home to my landlord's gift and note, there is also a series of voicemail messages. My ex is on a business trip, he announces. Then: on a whim, he's transferred at Bakersfield to a Capitol-bound train. It'll be great to catch up, goes the third message. He'll pull in at 8:30 PM, he adds.

Then the fourth: His next call will be from the station. If I am serious about leaving, he says, I need to tell him face-to-face.

I register the forced lightness. He is trying hard to sound as if we were on decent terms. That he has not made efforts to track me down, obtain my number. That our split ended with him wishing me well in my new life.

Despite myself, I'm moved by his effort. He hurt me. Also true: living without him is like somersaulting in space. I lack a significant fraction of every sense. Invisible in this hot and landlocked city, I am an outline of a person.

I'd visited the women's bookstore and cafe near my apartment with butterflies in my chest—this female-centered bastion was one reason I chose the neighborhood—but had been snapped at to close the door before the cat escaped. Wanting to make it up, I'd made a fuss over the obese feline, but the clerk had ignored me.

Now it is nearly 8:30. I sit at the edge of the pool, smoking my doobie. I swish my legs in the sun-warmed water. The bank of windows faces the pool, so despite the heat, I also wear my 60s-style fringed suede jacket. "The Hide," my ex had called it in friendlier times. Televisions come on. Manure perfumes the air.

The apartment lights begin to burn yellow. It's getting cold. I'm hungry. Inside, my frozen dinners are melting on the kitchen counter. But I stay in my bathing suit and The Hide, gently churning the water as though all thoughts have left my mind. That I haven't noticed the descending dark. The sound, again and again, from inside my apartment. My telephone's ring, punching the air

THE GHOST OF CHARLES BUKOWSKI PINES FOR HIS JOB AT THE MAILS

Death has done wonders for Hank's cratered face. His diarrhea and bellyache, gone.

The ghost of Charles "Hank" Bukowski rests in his lawn chair. His writing room is upstairs with its view of the industrial harbor. The room's long been done over as a nursery. Hank has no wish to rattle the young mother inside.

He really doesn't miss drinking. Doesn't miss writing. The women. All those sad parties. Rather, he yearns for the bourgeois pleasures of watching a kid from the block heaving the push mower east to west. He scratches his ghostly balls and relaxes into the salaryman's fantasia: a sweating pitcher of lemonade he and the boy could share. A neighboring family to hate. A steak defrosting on the counter.

Longs, in fact, for his old job at the Post Office. For a place to get up and dressed and rush to. A busted-up Wilmington sidewalk, wolf-toothed dogs behind cyclone fences. His aching feet. A rolling stool. A bank of letterboxes. The dragging clock. His jackass supervisor. Something to rail against.

His given name was Charles, but he went by Hank. One or two of the women who climbed through his bedroom window called him that, Charles. Seeking to distinguish themselves in his pickled, smeary mind.

Charles is the name from his paystub at the PO. Back in his mail sorter days, he had an apartment on Angel's Flight. He'd emulated the writer John Fante, the way callow young men now emulate him. Leaving bottles of rum at his grave. Charles. Hank. Buk. The plainspoken artiste who chucked the security of a government job.

The ghost of Charles Bukowski doesn't miss feeling like shit every morning, freezing his nuts off delivering mail, or those idiot acolytes knocking on his door.

He dreams, when he dreams, of those letters in his hands. A straight part in his hair. A friendly barber with a stack of girly magazines. His view of Terminal Island—Fante once called it home—across the harbor; halfway to Long Beach.

The ghost of Charles Bukowski rises weightless from his lawn chair. He hopes the neighbors don't complain about the shaggy lawn. His gravestone says, Don't try. But it features the image of a boxer, dukes up.

THE ALTOGETHER

Come to find out, Gina's co-worker's privates were damp looking. City slicker genitals. With sand veiling down from the hills above, Ned and Gina stood to move her serape and their things. "I feel like I'm in a monster movie," Ned muttered.

Oh, this was bad. Inviting him here had been a big mistake.

Gina and Ned had had four conversations up to today. He had told her he did walking meditation during the lunch break, and when he explained what that was, Gina said she did that too. People at work all thought Ned was gay. When Gina asked him about that, he said he wasn't. Also, that he had a son, Harry, who stayed with him alternating weeks. Gina now also knew that Ned had a small banner tattooed on his forearm, the name "Harry" scrollworked inside.

It was true that Gina liked to read and sleep at a nude beach. She'd eat her sandwich and her Flamin' Hot Cheetos. Nap. She had a tan butt and boobs. A pretty spray of roses tattooed on her arm. It was also true that Gina was lonely. She had a need to connect. She was trying to put a plan into action. A plan to stop doing everything by herself. She hadn't dated since moving back to Los Angeles a year before.

The grit mist of sand drifting down was from a wiry guy picking his way down the trail. He wore a fanny pack and sneakers. The fanny pack covered his penis but not his testicles, which were low-slung in that old-guy way. On his head with one hand, he balanced a cardboard flat of soda.

Ned put his underpants back on, green bikini-style. Then he and Gina came together, each holding two corners of her orange serape, minuet-style. Ned gave a little smile that was slightly devastating in that he seemed to be trying not to smile.

In the most mundane situations—usually with the very old or with an avuncular cashier—Gina often wondered what would happen if she leaned in for a kiss. It is not always because she was attracted to them; just more of a "what if?"

But she was.

Attracted to Ned.

"Is this weird?" she ventured. She reached for her sarong. Stopped herself. Her pulse banged. Ned regarded the sea.

"I don't know why I said that about the monster movie," he said. "I just feel this sense of . . . foreboding." He whispered the last word.

"So, the sight of naked people is creepy, or . . .?" Was it her? It was her.

"Maybe being here in the altogether, even though I'm not, really."

The altogether!

"It's a lull, but a stuffed lull," he said. "Like when I was seven." The two reset the serape and things.

"My older brother and I shared a bunk bed," Ned continued. "I had bottom. One night I woke up. I thought calmly, 'I need to move over right next to the wall, so when the bed breaks, I won't get smashed.'"

"What happened?" Now they were lying on their stomachs. Ned's legs were bent at the knees, crossed at the ankles.

"Well, I pressed myself to the wall and then Teddy's bunk crashed down."

"You . . . lived?" Gina asked. Ned smiled, shifted to his side so he could wiggle back out of his underwear.

Gina was okay with being naked in front of strangers. It was eye-to-eye contact that made her legs shake. Around them, the volleyball game, the gulls, the soda guy kneeling beside a trio of young women, all seemed a layer removed.

It was only naked Gina and her naked co-worker. Whose underwear sat in a little wad beside their sandwiches on the blanket between them.

Ned chewed his sandwich and watched the soda salesman, who was making his way over to the volleyball game. Those sodas had surely lost their chill.

"A NICE monster movie," he murmured. His mouth is much closer to her ear than she expected. She could smell the peanut butter on his breath.

"The IT guy," Gina intoned in a movie announcer voice. "He appeared to be a regular office person. Kept to himself."

"Can the movie poster be a shot of a guy with crazy hair? With his shirt buttoned to the collar, staring at the camera with mouth and eyes open wide?"

"With the faces of the various office types, in circles around him? Of course. It's the rule."

A shadow fell across them. It was the soda guy. He was deeply stoned, Gina saw. He apologized for bothering them and asked if they were thirsty. "Got any Cactus Cooler?" Ned asked. The soda guy looked crestfallen. "Just messing with you—we'll have a couple of Cokes."

Gina liked that Ned didn't dither or ask her first. He didn't assume Gina would want diet, or eschew soda. Ned gave the guy a couple of bills and the guy ambled off to where the sodas were, in the shade near the volleyball game.

Gina sat up—her tanned belly and breasts so close to Ned's face, but sometimes you have to say, oh what the hell—and reached for a sandwich.

She smiled at the soda guy. He said for Gina to have herself a marvelous day. Ned smiled at her. Brushed some grit from her arm.

And now they were inside a tender moment. Gina pictured Ned's tattoo, but instead of the "Harry," the banner read, "Kiss." His face was so close to hers that he appeared slightly cross-eyed.

And it was like a monster movie after all, but not the part with the monster in it. Instead, it was the part at the very end when after going through all the peril and running around, the hero and the soft, attractive gal were face to face, breathless. Altogether.

And then at last, they kissed.

"I know you're gay," Gina said.

For a moment, Ned said nothing. Then, "It's even better. We can really be friends. And we never have to break up." And he kissed her again, chastely. And he spanked her rear. And he was right. Because they remained the best of friends until the end of their days.

TRUST

Cherished Patty! I cover you with a cape of protection. We watch it float to your shoulders. I gaze on your reflection in my round mirror splashed with keepsakes my other friends have brought me from their vacations in New Orleans and Las Vegas and the Holy Land. I know you think they are cheap and tacky. I know you photograph my decor when I am around the corner, mixing your hair coloring. You text the photos to your friends. Sometimes I go out and have a smoke. You are happy playing with your mobile phone.

Then I stand behind you and grasp your hair, splaying it out and scratching your head as though you are my beloved cat. I urge you to remove your earrings, placing them on the narrow counter in front of my mirror. I ooh and aah at your turquoise or amber. I lift and remove your thick-lensed eyeglasses, so the chemicals will not harm their stems.

I amuse you with stories of my youth in the Ukraine. How I would try new things with my hair for novelty's sake, like shaving back my hairline or sporting cornrows, or dying it the matte black of a charcoal briquette. I tell you about the time I dyed my hair a volatile red, so stylish! It was for my only trip home, 15 years back. How I arrived at the airport and all the Ukrainian ladies wore their hair the same fox-red shade.

I am helping you grow your hair out and lightening it over time. You joke that you are trying to look like me. But you do not know my looks; not the way I know yours, Patty. I know your skull, your hairline. That weird curly patch. I know about your affair. Without your eyeglasses, you cannot see. We have that trust.

I am aware you have seen the fleshy growths on the back of my head. The ones I cover with my honey-hued waves. I registered your shock before you averted your eyes.

I soothe your fears when you come to me, in a whirl over the latest thing President Trump has broadcasted on social media. I give you Russian tea. I give you samples of products good for your baby-fine hair. I give you a chunk of honeycomb. I wrap it for you in aluminum foil, twisted into the shape of a swan. You take a photo of me proffering it. It never occurs to you I'll see it on Instagram.

You just love to keep up on the news. The day of that terrible fire in the Russian mall, you ask me what I think. You have tears in your eyes. I tell you it was definitely worse than you think.

Way back when, you may have actually heard about Chernobyl before I did. I was there for the people lifting their babies up to see the weirdly beautiful light. But what I am saying is, you might have heard the truth.

This is what is, was, to be Ukrainian. Throw yourself dreamless on the fire. Defend. Sacrifice. Dread is something inside of us, Patty. Like a ghost I and my countrymen harbor. A full day after Chernobyl, volunteers appeared, to shampoo the streets. From behind our curtains, we watched in our robes. Over and over, this happened, in the early mornings. Shampooing and shampooing.

Hand mirror aloft, I spin you with care and tell you that if anything, your hair is thicker.

RAT GIRL

She calls herself Rat Girl, but she looks like a little Swiss doll. Now in the Chapel, she is singing round-eyed over our heads and serpentine-ing her head in the shape of infinity as she always does. Her arms are sinewy, pounding at her guitar; bracketing small breasts in a tiny pink t-shirt.

Now she is reading from her book, about that time when she was hit by a car. How afterward she saw her reflection in a Good Samaritan's mirrored sunglasses. How she saw her own blazing eyes in a bloody mass of meat. Then she puts the book away and the sound of her singing tears the air between us again.

All four of us are standing at the side of the sanctuary-turned-performance space. It's me, Trinidad, Blaze, and Michael. All of us are old fans. Because of Rat Girl's wiseacre patter, the intimacy of her lyrics, and her frankness in interviews, people feel they know her well. She is small and bright-eyed and has suffered many hardships, so thousands of people over the land would like to take care of her. I myself am a middle-aged married woman who wishes to lick her biceps, strum her neck tendons. "Get in line, Mama Cat," I imagine her saying in that cactus dirt rasp.

Michael brings more drinks, and Rat Girl sings about the notion of spurning. What am I spurning by scribbling notes on the backs of business cards during this performance in this room, its ship bottom ceiling illuminated by purple light? Why push Rat Girl away by snapping a blurry photo with my cell phone? On my third glass of vodka, dulling her potency? She is too strong for me. The details of her life, too dark.

Rat Girl's husband has recently left her, I know. She has endured dissociative disorder, the kidnapping of one of her children by his father, the suicide of her best friend. She tours constantly, like any brilliant artist without a record contract. Her lyrics are crystalline. Members of the audience shut their eyes, overcome.

What happens after you realize the members of your support group are dead? Rat Girl asks us near the end of the show. Do you keep yearning for them, or do you dig in where you are? Her eyes are still bright. She makes these questions sound wry rather than tragic. Maybe that is why she is so beloved.

The show is over. Thank you very much, Rat Girl says, and while it does not sound earnest, she is a 100% earnest woman and the real deal. She reads a little more from the book she wrote, this time about a bus ride that into a crime scene when she was "a hundred years pregnant." She swears to all of us it's a pretty funny book, and that she doesn't die in the end. Then she adds that she hopes she isn't spoiling it.

After the concert, we walk with Blaze and Michael to the 16th street BART. The iron Day of the Dead tree grates have all been installed on steel and glass Valencia Street. But Mission looks exactly the same to me as when I lived in this neighborhood years ago.

Perhaps inspired by Rat Girl, Michael tells a story about almost losing his arm. It seems that earlier this month, he contracted some kind of flesh-eating bacteria, which led to a terrible infection. We are passing that liquor store that sells cards and dice. It is on the corner, and if you were to walk straight forward through the door, you would ram into a pillar.

Then the Roxie Theater, then *Esta Noche,* that drag bar where Michael's friend used to perform as Diana Ross.

The night is crisp. Trinidad crooks his arm, and I take it. The red brick 16th and Mission Plaza are lined with sleeping people. Blaze and Michael are laughing their asses off about the flesh-eating bacteria, so we laugh, too. Inside, we laugh and laugh, avoiding one another's tired eyes in the white-lit subway car. Across San Francisco, under the Bay, and back to our warm apartments and humming appliances and dozing pets who come alive at the sound of the key in the lock.

COUNTRY MUSIC

An unsmiling Lyft driver with kohl-outlined eyes brought me up 17th Street to Saturn. Seeing me, she mashed her radio button to country. The fare seemed too meager to deliver me to my husband, who's been working in California for seven weeks now. San Francisco, with all those hills and sidewalks and garage doors.

An hour later, my husband's small room cannot contain our misery. He suggests taking the dog outside. He is ready first. I dip to tie my shoe, my shoulders still feeling the imprint of his dry hands. His shoulders have broadened. It's the swimming, he said. He goes to an outdoor pool. He sighs from the hallway. Now I understand: He didn't plan on having me join the walk.

One of our big differences: Rather than run, I suck on misery as if its marrow sustains me.

He didn't have to accept this gig. His company is making changes, but our home branch is staying. In this "post-pandemic" world where work models will change forever, businesses are strategizing changes. So are workers. "Making life choices," I overheard him say to his boss. Before this move to San Francisco, he worked remotely from our living room. As an RN, my "work model" only added layers of personal protective equipment, safety precautions, and stress-related hair loss.

My cup of wine tips. I use my husband's white underpants—he's begun wearing boxer briefs—to mop the red mess. I call out: Go on; I'll start some dinner.

I know this man. He is already thinking ahead to where his new dog will deposit his excrement. Pondering the color and consistency. It is getting dark outside. Strong-jawed men are stepping down 17th street to the Castro, smelling fine. My husband will be crouched, shining his cell phone flashlight to check his dog's leavings.

I leave his sodden underpants in the corner, under a towel. After I am gone, my husband will find them. The red stain will make him believe he has a terrible disease. That something seeps from him while he dwells so far away from me and our apartment in icy brick Boston.

This is not our home. Obviously, nothing magical remains. But the fibers of my husband's briefs are marked by meager mystery. It's nothing, but it's all I have. He will be scared, and then ultimately all right.

Backstroke. Butterfly. Crawl. Introducing the dog around at the office, which he has described as "open concept."

I will be far but ever-present, a ghost with unfinished business. I will never let him move on.

THE OTHER SUSANA

My husband and I sit in folding chairs at the Café de Nord, thighs touching. The Burlap Slackers are a husband-and-wife cowpunk act. Wild West types in red velvet and corduroy. The husband has one of those syrupy, bottomless baritones. I mean, I could just tip my chair into that voice and disappear.

Ostensibly we are companionable, but the last thing I said to my husband before the show started was if he wasn't going to do a thing to help, he could stop patting me all the damn time.

The tech bros in the audience continue to talk, giving no sign they are aware the show has begun. Reminding me: Things are going badly with our son. Thor is 20 and living in South America. His texts are infrequent but specific. Here is a photo of the redheaded, size-zero mother of his girlfriend, who is "an actual grifter!" Now, he is writing a choose-your-own-adventure book about his drug dealing experiences. Now he is breaking up with his girlfriend. Now he needs money for rehab. At home, a hole remains in the wall above our fireplace. I have covered the hole with an oil painting of a sea captain I bought at Thrift Town. But I have left visible the daubs of blood on the mantle. I have not erased the words, "Fuck off" in pencil on the brick hearth.

My husband gives me a happy little punch on the arm and sucks back the last of his 7&7. The Burlap Slackers really are so good. Between songs, the singer, Susana Felton, tells the audience about the courtyard complex where they lived in Philadelphia. That winter, she says, there was always some crazy person or another in the courtyard, yelling in their underpants. Now she and her husband live in the tallest building in Bisbee, Arizona, she says. The house's turrets are sharpened to razor points.

There are two Susanas. The one at work is a waxy-skinned girl Thor's age, the receptionist. This morning, she told me she went through two canisters of asthma inhaler her first week at work. On Susana's first day, HR issued an e-mail memo to the staff, reminding us that we have a scent-free workplace.

And yet those bitches from finance still descend upon our conference room each Tuesday morning in a veritable cartoon cloud of perfume. This has made me protective of Reception Susana. Today when I entered the office, I smelled something pleasant and familiar. Tea tree oil, she told me. She was spraying down all the cubes with it, using a small plastic spray bottle. Tea tree oil, alcohol, and water. The alcohol kills dust mites! Was I allergic to dust mites? No?

I told her about my husband's asthma, and about how it's really kicked up since I can't stop rearranging our furniture. We should replace our pillows every six months, Rennie told me. She also recommended a lamp I should buy, a special pink one made of salt.

After the show, the glamorous Susana Felton sits at the merch table with her husband, hawking CDs, shirts, and her original paintings. All of the paintings are of forest animals. Up close you can see the circles under Susana's eyes from all the traveling. You can smell her healthy sweat. She confides that if they'd known San Francisco was so close to the water, they never would have come. "Right now, we're surrounded by octopus," she pouts. Her baritone husband whistles through his teeth, just like my Grandma Estelle. He confides to us that squirrels are stealing his pills.

"Do you have a hard time getting refills?" my kind husband asks him. And in the fraction of a second that follows, I see a kind of gratitude in Susana's and the baritone's eyes. She takes care of him. He needs her.

Reception Susana has told me she plans to arrive at tomorrow's holiday party in a glittery sweater with big fake birds clipped to it. The finance staff will be dressed alike in red and green. They will watch from their flowery nimbus of scents, their smoky eyes like arrow tips.

Again and again I will excuse myself—in motherhood's terror and unconditional despair—for the ladies' room, where I will thumb my phone open to search for a scrap of evidence that our child is alive. Yes, I will do this thing.

But I will also throw myself on the sword to protect Reception Susana. I will squire her to the food table and ensure she gets the best of the Safeway cheese 'n' lunch meat platter. I will tell her which Secret Santa gift to choose. Position the two of us to disrupt the background of all the selfies those finance housecats take.

I will let my hands hover over Susana's bird-bedecked shoulders. I will channel my inner mother hawk, beholden to no archer.

NOT NOWADAYS, AND NEVER HERE

What day is it; is Whit still with her? It's Comfrey's habit to ask herself these questions whenever she awakes. And of course, she and Whit are not at home. Her husband and she are staying at an Airbnb, a kind of vacation rental whose "hosts" are the homeowners themselves.

Comfrey is here to give a lecture. She reserved this place when it became clear it was too late to book a room at the conference hotel. She was roped in by a photo of an unspoiled beach, another of small boats docked prettily together. What it boils down to is, she has accidentally rented a room two hours' drive from where the conference is being held.

"Your son is away at college, I presume?" Comfrey had asked, and the host—a dour, exhausted-looking woman—had hesitated, then nodded.

It had been a long drive to the Airbnb, passed mainly in silence, Comfrey drinking in what sights she could from the passenger side window. The sky was an inverted iron bowl above. The air was velvety with a faint sour smell. The birds would be completely different here.

Comfrey is here to give a talk, a paper, at the conference, yes, that's it. She'd bungled the travel plans. They'd almost missed the plane.

Bidar means awake. Comfrey has always been fond of saying it. Last night, she told the Iranian Ubercar driver en route to this place that Bidar is her last name and asked, was it true that Bidar means awake in Persian?

The nightgown she has brought for this trip is sleeveless and black and slinky, with a big purple flower at the bottom. Funnily enough, it makes Comfrey think of her mother. Now that she herself is past sixty, Comfrey's body echoes her mother's in its pale bulk. So maybe she does not like this nightgown after all. She rises and stands unmoving. Her hips must adjust to the holding of her. She is doing exactly what her mother used to do.

Whit always wakes up early no matter when he gets to sleep. He fixes his coffee and then leaves it to grow cold. Then he takes his morning walk. He hums as he goes and waves at everyone he sees. He will have seen the new birds. When he returns, he will heat his coffee in the microwave and chat with the host. He always enjoys coffee standing, along with his protein bar, the kind cyclists keep in their small saddlebags. He used to save her one; when had that small offering ended?

It is like Comfrey to accept what is offered. Like this room, painted pale green with heavy drapes and a small sink. Like Whit himself, accompanying her like an attentive chaperone, yet leaving her to arrange the bookings, the Ubercar. He won't even listen to Comfrey give her talk. He is not that kind of husband. He'll be outside, dressed in his salmon trousers and white fedora hat, chatting up the workers at the conference center. Or across the street, ordering his new drink, a terrible seltzer that is flavored with synthetic fruit and contains alcohol.

When Comfrey had asked the Ubercar driver about their name, the driver said yes. Yes, bidar does mean awake, but it's a word you only hear in old poetry. Not nowadays, and never here.

And then she begins to laugh. Of course, Whit is not here at all! It's all so silly, her trickster brain. She'll check her emails.

But when she sits, the single bed is wet, and so is the hem of her pretty nightgown, and so are her feet. She has had another accident. She slips out of the gown and tries to use it to blot the mattress. And that is the moment that Whit appears in the doorway, the sun behind him. He *is* here. Dressed in matching jade-colored top and trousers. Those weird squishy sandals. Named after crocodiles, mystifyingly.

But it is not Whit at all, Comfrey realizes, but a pale-blue-masked young man. Slim and smiling. Reaching for her. This is his room, she understands. And it strikes Comfrey, in this small room alone so far from home, that something unpleasant is coming her way—wherever she might go—with a slow and inescapable resolve.

SO YOU THINK YOU CAN TELL

His new doctor is Doogie Howser, my father tells me over lunch. "Barely out of short pants." My mom gives an appreciative chuckle.

"They're all Doogie Howser now," I say.

I am staying with my parents. My mom and dad have been married for 49 years. I'd believed my marriage was the long-lasting kind, too. There was no Plan B.

Our meal finished, I wave them away and started clearing the dishes. My dad touches my mom's shoulder as they head to their separate locations.

Shelter-in-Place has barely caused a ripple in their routines. My mom is in the guest room, doing her medical transcription. Because I live here for the first time in decades, I now know that for years she cried every time She Blinded Me with Science came on the oldies station, because Thomas Dolby was my favorite in high school. On the mantle is a photo of me in a wide-shouldered, double-breasted jacket and those round flip-up sunglasses. My hair permed in front like a rockabilly heartthrob.

My dad's where he always is, in the garage sitting behind the wheel of his parked 1974 Gran Torino, his dog Ben riding shotgun. My father and old Ben enjoy Pink Floyd. How many times have I heard him croon Shine on You Crazy Diamond into Ben's velvet ears?

Doctors *are* getting younger. Funnily enough, my new ophthalmologist is an old guy. It's the departing one—with her shiny curls and fat cheeks and two babies at home—who was Doogie Howser. The old guy is only filling in, the tech told me as she prepared the eye chart setup. They'd grab one just out of school for much cheaper, she explained. More energy, she said.

I was surprised to see the substitute wasn't very old at all. He looked like Thomas Hayden Church in Sideways. I wondered if he knew he wasn't getting the gig. He turned the dials expertly. Briskly aimed the piercing light into the backs of my eyeballs to peek at my optic nerve. Pressure's 17 in each, he sighed. He didn't possess the vim and pep of my old ophthalmologist in her Laura Petrie capris and ballet flats. But 17 meant we forestalled the surgical option another year.

"Come back in four months," Thomas Hayden Church said, then stopped himself from adding, "See you then." His blue eyes were tired above his mask. I thought I saw the outline of contact lenses. I knew he wasn't Thomas Hayden Church in Sideways. But I still saw him delivering the news that he wasn't hired, and his wife bashing him with her motorcycle helmet like Sandra Oh in the movie. How I wanted to tell him to take a load off in the exam chair! We could close the door and pretend he was still helping me; he could get some rest. I'd sit in his lap if he thought it would help.

I squirt Lemon Joy over the breakfast and lunch dishes, then wait for the sink to fill. Now that our son has graduated from college, my husband says he is ready to "start his third act." He has earned a fresh start, he told me. He is excited to shed his life like an old patchwork coat and walk away to a bright-lit studio apartment with no closets and one brick wall as if on stage at an intimate club. That's what landed me here at my parents' condo. Back when we met, he'd been a tankini of boyfriends: two different parts that went together. A sensitive guy who worked construction. On the job we were two lost souls, reading poetry together at lunch. Swimming in a fishbowl of our coworkers' wisecracks. I knew without our ever having discussed it, that as long as I was willing to face them, our romance was a go.

That's when it comes: A hideous skid and crunch from outside. Metallic and final. The condo faces a wide street just a few yards from a big intersection. Crashes are not unheard of. In this surreal time of quarantine, absolutely nothing outside of this house would surprise me.

The condo stays quiet. I consider: I'd so much rather be in a crash than to witness one, with no way to help. When I had our son, I was pleased to bear the pain, with my husband there to serve as wowed onlooker.

The thin wail of sirens thickens and intensifies. The neighbors are emerging. My mother, I realize, wears headphones for her transcription. That is why she hasn't come to investigate.

I run. Outside, the cries of birds are deafening. Everything outside is just so damn loud.

Then I see it: the accident. My father's Gran Torino has rolled backward into traffic. His side of the car is mashed. I rush to the passenger side and reach over the old dog, Ben. My father's eyes are open but unfocused.

Music spills through the speakers. Wish You Were Here. His favorite. The sirens, earsplitting by now, abruptly cut off. The EMTs burst out in paper gowns, gloves, clear face shields, and masks underneath. Doogie Howsers, all. My face is naked, I realize. The EMTs approach.

Under my body, the dog Ben whimpers. I avert my head and breathe until my throat opens up again.

"Take my strength," I implore my father. My bare arms buzz, surging as though tapped with a naked wire. "Take it,

Dad. Hurry." Above the windshield, electric lines cross like the mast and lines of a sailboat against the blue sky.

One of the Doogie Howsers is saying—I cannot gauge their expression behind the veil of their face shield, the mask—that I really, really need to get out of the way.

ANTWERP ZOO SAYS WOMAN WHO HAD 'AFFAIR' WITH CHIMP MUST STAY AWAY FOR 'HIS HEALTH'

The so-called experts simper that a chimpanzee who is seen as being too close to humans is less respected by his peers. Like I care what those knuckle draggers think. Blonde Carol, my love, is facing empty nest syndrome. This had led from one thing to another and at this point, her children have blocked her on all the socials. Her texts go unanswered, and she receives no thanks for the baked goods she leaves.

Until today, my sweet consort would visit me daily in this most virtual of places. I mean, think about it. I am literally enclosed here. She was made to pay money to access my company. Carol would wave and blow me kisses; jump up and down. We never touched. She broke no rule. All I wanted was to cradle, to protect her.

Antwerp Zoo Says Woman Who Had 'Affair' with Chimp Asked to Stay Away for 'His Health,' the headline smirked. Oh, I saw. And now my life is scrubbed of both my peers' respect and my *amour fou* with my soul's twin.

My family is gone, too.

IN THE MIDST OF A GLOBAL PANDEMIC, YOUR WASHING MACHINE GIVES UP THE GHOST

Just like the garbage disposal and floor heater. Before you were laid off, it was tough to break from work to await a workman's long window. Today it's a feat to scramble the quarters for this long-postponed trip to the laundromat.

You tell yourself you'll wait in the car during the cycles. You've "sheltered" alone for nine months. You stay. It's hot inside, like in your childhood, far away. The same humid air. The banks of molded orange chairs; the ceiling-mounted TV. The dried-thin softener sheets littering cement floors.

Two young women chat about a double date after church on Sunday. Their eyes are merry above their masks. The clothes they fold are sweet and bright. Beside you, a man in a nylon soccer shirt slumps nearly prone, finger pecking his phone. You don't normally appreciate men's cologne, but his somehow smells delicious.

That famous San Francisco chocolate is actually made in your town of overflowing trash cans, nail salons, and lumpy sidewalks. The factory's half a mile from this laundromat. Even closer to the emergency room. The smell of fresh confection perfumes the most unpretty places.

The ceiling-mounted TV issues the news. The volume swells. The nearby casino blares wide-grinning winners. "You could be next." There's a sale-a-bration at "your" Acura dealer. Your county's experiencing a historic mass exodus.

When the timer buzzes, you shove hot frayed towels, laundered-thin t-shirts, into pillowcases. Your underpants cling to everything like starfishes.

It isn't true that your washing machine has given up the ghost. It's not broken at all. You've just been hunkered down alone for so long in your small apartment, where nothing is broken but things inside of you have begun to stop working.

A father swings his giggling baby so the little one's bare toes tap the buttons of the vending machine. He catches your eye and you both smile under your masks. You tilt your head and crinkle your eyes, so he'll know. The door chimes and you all turn to check out the new arrival.

CHALK OUTLINE

5:10 p.m. The downtown lights gleamed hard in the frigid air. Slouched behind the wheel, Vic watched as Loretta's staff—the few whose physical presence was deemed "essential"—broke at the lobby door and hunched to their cars.

Loretta, gone for 15 business days now. Working remote from her sister's place in Syracuse. Without her presence enlivening the air, Vic's apartment's old odors had returned. The sheets smelled like his dirty hair. Lorettta's presence, her belongings, had given the place life.

Weekends, Vic did okay. It was practically sanctioned to fill the hours with TV and gin. During the week, he'd begun taking his dinner here, at Loretta's workplace. And he'd cut down on the drinking. A shot or two before bed and that was it. A routine helped.

He ran for it, sliding a little on the ice. A swipe of Loretta's badge and he was inside. She'd left her work keys behind in an old hoodie of Vic's.

In the company break room, he got a fresh pot of coffee going. The earthy smell of dripping French roast made Vic feel like a diary opened to a creamy blank page.

He'd reverted to eating in the manner of the always-alone: noisily and too fast. Only tonight, the communal refrigerator was empty. The same old crusted mustard, unloved salad dressings. Pimiento-stuffed olives and gummy jam. He'd need to cross a new line: check desk drawers for sustenance.

He began moving briskly from station to station. Spied cheap mementos from tropical honeymoons and package vacays. Ointments and plaque-spattered dental supplies. In IT Calvin's cable-filled drawer, a deck of cards. Vic tucked it into his jacket pocket.

Bingo. Old Mel, accounts receivable, kept a bottle of good whiskey in the back of his filing cabinet. The company Christmas gift from two years back. A glittery card was still taped to the label. Vic sucked a mouthful, then another. Better. Good.

Reasoning that Mel was less likely to notice the bottle's absence than he was to smell the open container, Vic brought the bottle to the break room. His hands glittered. He splashed whiskey into someone's pink "Yass, Kween!" mug, took a slug. A fine, syrupy feeling spread in his chest and limbs. He got an expired sack of microwave popcorn started.

He'd waited two long weeks to breach Loretta's office. She was the CEO, but she was also Vic's wife. Coming here had been a healing experience for Vic, he could tell. He felt good. Camera ready! He chuckled, flashing jazz hands.

He dance-walked back to the work space. Dumb Dahlia, he noticed, had littered her reception station with bride magazines. Vic and Loretta's own wedding and reception had been a potluck, held in a shabby Queen Anne managed by the Parks & Rec. It had been a sweet affair. Vic had drunk far too much, but Loretta had let it go. Let it go night after night in the months that followed, at least he'd thought so until it was too late.

In Dahlia's shallow left-hand drawer, he found a box of sample garters. Pastel green, peach, and blue. Confectionary hues nearly leached of color. Underneath the box, Vic found himself face-to-face with his own wedding album. Affixed to the cover was a Post-it, on which Loretta's handwriting said, "Keep it! No bother returning!!"

Vic's breath went shallow. Their smiles, his and Loretta's. The hopeful clothes. The faces of those happy guests. That cake. A sound like a cornered dog came from him then. He tore the photos from the album. They made a trail behind him as he stumbled to Loretta's office door.

But it was Loretta's scent that sent him reeling. Neroli: orange blossom. His legs went boneless. Vic gripped her gleaming desk as he sank to the floor.

It was so quiet he could hear the ticking of the microwave in the break room, where the popcorn had started bursting.

He removed his shirt. Spread it out on the carpet, splayed like a chalk outline. He used to be great at this. He slid the pack of playing cards from his pocket. Began to build a foundation. Triangular trusses were for amateurs. Vic worked quickly, building some height with squares and right angles. He still had it! The tower rose.

Suddenly: the jangling of keys. The door handle shook. Shook again. From his crouching position behind his house of cards, Vic heard a key entering the lock.

And registered the explosions of the popcorn kernels. Faster. Faster. Like a firing squad in a village so close to his own.

IN THE BACK YARD

It's five o'clock and already chilling. I started the sprinkler after lunch and then forgot. I half-hear the water streaming through the pipes, registering it more as a charge in the atmosphere than as an actual sound.

I get the sourdough toast going and spray the omelet pan with coconut oil. The smell of warming bread imparts normalcy and calm. I crack two brown eggs into the yellow bowl, then whisk in cubes of Swiss cheese and a little chopped spinach. When everything's done, I place a tea towel over my forearm and head outside.

Before he moved to the back yard and became a jacaranda tree, I was the one who spotted the blood on my husband Peter's t-shirts. The doctor told me Peter had to have ignored the lumps below his nipple for months.

Peter engaged with the doctor during the visit, nodding and taking down notes about the possibility of hormone treatment, chemo, and targeted therapy. It's just that he refused to keep the next appointment. And the next. By the end of the month, he'd moved outside. A week later, his toes had spread and inserted themselves into the earth. One day I returned from work to see that his body had become a lithe trunk. Soon, it darkened. Broadened. I know these leaves from my home country. Jacaranda.

I kick off my clogs, balancing the plate and glass of guava juice. The fork, I jam vertically into my bra. The food is for me. Peter is watered, not fed.

Biodegradable urns exist that convert you into a tree after you die. *Epidermodysplasia verruciformis* is an extremely rare skin condition that can cause bark-like growths.

This is not either of those things.

I step carefully, holding the plate aloft. The mud is cold under my bare feet. At the back of the yard stands the man I married. The sprinkler has created a silver pool at his base. Its spray catches the light.

We're having a cold snap. This is following a long warm spell, which fooled crocuses and daffodils into rising and opening far too early.

Nature has lost its train of thought.

I set the plate on the child-size bench. I sit down and eat my dinner. Then I open my blouse and bare my clavicle, my shoulders. This is how far things have come.

There was a time when Peter's kisses rubbed my face raw. When I'd lose minutes at work thinking of our intimate times. Late at night, his marine smell comforted me in our bed. The homey buzz of his snores lulled me as I drifted to sleep.

Across the yard, our home's windows begin to soften to gold. The water still moves through our pipes, making its keening sound.

A breeze comes and I believe I smell my husband's marine scent again. The green onion of his underarms. I trace his bark, brown-gray and mature. Deep clefted. My own hands are grooved with age. I wrap my arms around him, press my own soft trunk against his hardness. I raise my face and fill my eyes with the abundance of lavender-colored blooms against the dark branches, the purpling sky.

I feel his humming life force as I believe he feels mine. I need to believe it. The fact is, in recent months, ours was a lonely marriage. I'd make small gambits to capture his attention. Connect. Would experience tiny griefs when those gambits failed. I dissipated every time.

An untimely gust races frigid through the wide-open arms of his branches. Lavender flowers issue and rain onto the lawn, my bared shoulders.

The tremor begins between my thighs and grows until I'm clutching his trunk, legs weak. I say his name. Say it again.

Right now, it is enough; it is all the healing I need.

VELELLA VELELLA

This morning, my brothers and I battled the southbound eye-five freeway traffic in our mother's yellow Beetle. We are here because she might die. Subtract herself from this mortal coil. Last night in the emergency room, we witnessed her fighting for breath, eyes ablaze. The hospital personnel pushed into the tiny room. I wrote furiously everything I saw and heard. Rather than watching over like a proper daughter.

My older brother, the successful adult, has flown from Cleveland. He wears a button up shirt and sport coat. He demands that a nurse explain to him what the heck has just happened. And it turns out that what has happened is, the force that has governed every decision I've ever made was just ushered into a coma.

Every day in the ICU, my brothers and I wear purple rubber gloves and yellow paper gowns. Pretty early on, coarse hairs appear on our mother's chin. By the next visit they are gone. One day, our baby brother is there for it, and reports that the nurse shaves her "like a man." My successful brother asks to cut her fingernails and is informed mildly that a tiny nick could cause her to bleed to death.

My brothers and I low-key compete to see who can be the most helpful around her house. I recognize and am dispirited at our eagerness to please her even though she is unconscious. During our visits to the ICU, we report back to her on these homey tasks, with one another as audience. Between us, she lies like a fallen queen in her raised hospital bed, kept alive by medicines in draped tubes, and machines that rhythm and blink their activities in numbers only one of us—our baby brother the RN—understands.

One eye-smartingly bright day, the news comes that Michael Jackson has died. My brothers and I belt out his hits in the tiny car. Beat It. Billie Jean. Smooth Criminal. Everyone in my family sings, loudly and well. On the radio, people share their feelings. They are weeping over Michael Jackson and how happy he made them. The music returns. We turn up the volume and sing our asses off.

Back at her house, the hopeful details of our mother's life are displayed. Before her heart attack, she'd decorated for Easter. Inside her fireplace is an iron candelabra with never-used candles from the 99 Cents Store. Every evening, we light them all. I worry silently that I'll forget to purchase new ones before she returns home. We're all participating, but only I fear I will be blamed.

Upstairs in her closet, out-of-season clothing is tucked away in labeled boxes. Jackets, slacks, and blouses from her working days are hung according to color. Much of it, I'm dismayed to see, is in my size. I have always thought of my mother as a woman of great size. I begin wearing her shirts, then her hats. One June night, I descend the stairs in one of her nightgowns and my brothers stifle their laughter. I begin wearing her lime green Crocs instead of my Doc Martens. But the rubber clogs are too big, and always fly off while I walk.

In the ICU, we do things we would never dare in regular life. Like holding our mother's hand. Stroking her arm. Growing up, it was a given that she hated being touched. She comes from the generation that let infants "cry it out." She and her sister, Great Depression babies, were fed from bottles of Karo syrup mixed with water.

The nurse says it's important to talk to her, that studies have shown she can hear. It never occurred to me that she couldn't. We deliver for her sprightly narratives about our children, our home lives. She had little interest in such stories when she was well.

I need to keep up with my contract work. In her bedroom, I ease myself into her computer chair. The place where, before bed, she powers up her ten-year-old PC for online games of Hearts and Scrabble.

I cannot focus. From where I sit, I see:

- A Zip-lock baggie of graham crackers fashioned into sandwich cookies, peanut butter smeared between them.
- A handwritten list of all her passwords. The same handwriting as in our long-ago field trip permission slips and sick notes. All those birthday cards.
- In an unsealed envelope, her Last Will and Testament.

Oddest are the triangular shards of clear plastic strewn across her bedroom floor. I am afraid to move them. My mother lies comatose, 15 miles away, but the child inside me is sure I'll catch hell.

The plastic pieces remind me of that strange sea life you see from time to time on Pacific beaches: Velella velella. Sometimes called "By-the-Wind Sailors," these creatures normally inhabit the open ocean, using strands of stingers to snag tiny animals. I learn that although they are tiny, they are related to the Portuguese man-of-war. According to National Geographic, "If you touch them, you might not feel any pain in your fingers. But if you rub your eyes or touch a more sensitive part of your skin, you're going to feel it. The rule is: don't touch."

After a week it dawns on me: the plastic pieces were left behind by the EMTs when they entered my mother's bedroom and saved her life. I scoop them up and set them in the "Jack" bathroom sink, powdery with disuse. That's when I spy it on the floor near her low dresser: the torn-open blister pack of nitroglycerine.

One morning at the ICU, I glimpse her leg, the skin leatherlike where they performed the angioplasty. Rough stitches draw the flesh together. Football, I think foolishly.

Medicineplus.gov says: "To reach the vein, a surgical cut will be made along the inside of your leg, between the ankle and groin. One end of the graft will be sewn to the coronary artery." Then oddly adds, "The procedure is performed while the heart is still beating."

In July, when she is conscious and has been transferred to rehab in La Jolla, she will provide us with driving directions to all her favorite second hand stores and libraries. The second-run movie theater that gives seniors free popcorn and sometimes a poster. She will ask for a seafoam cardigan from home. She will know precisely where it is.

In August, she will ask me to purchase some small items for her homecoming. She'll be sitting up in her bed in a t-shirt and adult diaper. After four months, she knows exactly what she needs. She knows the exact amount of money is folded into the side pocket of her purse.

There in the rehab, an old Aldo Ray movie blares from the wall television. I feel the burden of her measured gaze. I feel like she is daring me to say there might be another amount in her wallet.

That night in her darkened bedroom, I'll brush my teeth in the "Jill" sink. As I open her purse, my breaths will come fast like those of a bungling robber. Of course, she is right about the amount of cash she has there. When I marvel, she says, "Well, for me, it has only been a few days."

For five months, we crisscross the sky from our separate homes and lives. Keep our work lives afloat. Our mother's house remains flung open for inhabitation, investigation. A cutaway home. Like her own body during that time of procedures and body parts being updated, refreshed. When we all melt away, we keep the front door key hidden in the place we have established: under a backyard statue of a fox.

TO THE WOMAN PACING IN CIRCLES IN FRONT OF THE ELEMENTARY SCHOOL, HER FRESH-GROOMED DOG TROTTING ALONGSIDE

The morning is as crisp as your purebred's summer cut. My eyes smart from the sun-blasting chrome of rear-view mirrors. The children have been ushered inside the elementary school, trailing vinyl lunch pails and juice boxes and bright pandemic masks. The working mothers in their smart shoes have zoomed off. The stay-at-homes have vanished for errands, or neighborhood walks in clots of threes and fours before heading home to stuffed laundry hampers, for meat to defrost. These days my husband and I work at home. In these lockdown months, we have leapt forward in age.

You pace your terse circles. I approach with Owen, my hyper-social mutt.

At first, I think you are on a call. But you are talking yourself down. That's when I know you could be me, twenty years back. Having handed my son to his teacher, to the teeming lunchtime and the impossible stretch of green field. When he was a toddler, I'd have nightmares of him crying alone on that expanse.

I would have been scrambling, late for work. My husband and I tag-teamed. We never did let our son walk the short distance alone. By the time he was ten, he hated us for that.

You, the pacing woman, take deep and shaking breaths. My instinct is to give you privacy. Owen has another idea. He's straining at his leash, wiggling his whole bottom half. About six feet away from you, he plants himself on the sidewalk and waits.

Similarly, your purebred remains focused on you. Neither he nor you notice my magical dog, whose gaze is like a tunnel to solace.

I worried ceaselessly about my son, and it still all came to a terrifying head. We lost him. He was an adult, but my child, my joy. The whole world lost him. Oh, but now is not the time to tell you those stories. I will tell you another one, a more uplifting one.

When our son was just a toddler, we visited a new park across town. And he vanished from my sight, for not more than a couple of minutes, but of course I was terrified. The park was beside the old veterans building. Beside the building was a sort of breezeway where the dumpsters were. We passed that alcove entering the park and my son saw a rat atop the dumpster. And then I pushed him on the swings, and he climbed the stairs to the slide and all of that and got distracted, looking back at the dumpster and thinking about the rat. And I lost her. Only for a couple of minutes. I ran to my son and scooped him up, held him tightly to me.

An older woman was sitting on one of the park benches. She clucked and said, "You never stop worrying about them." And I asked, "oh . . . how old is yours?" And she'd said, 30, which seemed so funny to me back then.

For years I lost myself in work by day, in worry at night. I'd be pacing, racing my thoughts lacing, knotting, choking. Hearing the train at its appointed hours, the last and then the first subway car of the night and then the day. Dashing out of work to take him to the doctor, to the therapist. Sneaking out to throw dinner groceries into a market cart. What would I have done back then, confronted by a deep-eyed mutt and a smiling woman in purple scarves? Would I have noticed? Or would I do as you are doing now, continue pacing as if alone in pre-grieving?

Your loyal pet matches your pace, stops when you do. Goes again. I want to cup your elbows in my warm palms, exchange four air kisses, French-style. I'd clench my jaw a little, so you could feel my strength. And then I would say, in a voice so gentle, "Man, who did I think I was, thinking that torturing myself would keep my child bound to me and safe?"

Scruffy Owen hasn't taken his eyes from you. He'll wait here all day. Wait for you to see him, and notice. Will you accept? He will wait all day, until you look. He will lean. And then shift so he is sitting right atop your feet.

LOCATION

My dry cleaner proposed to me in the parking lot at El Matador Beach, over Malibu Country Mart's second cheapest bottle of prosecco. As we sat on a bench in the blufftop parking lot. Me, queasy from the motorcycle ride.

Leon worked in the basement of a Century City skyscraper. Fourteen floors above, I answered phones. So far, we had gone on three dates, if you count walking his elderly bulldog as two of them. For this fourth date, I'd gotten a mani-pedi in French Raspberry at the ritzy salon over the little pedestrian bridge from the office. With my short fingernails, my hands looked like a pageant toddler's.

Now Leon took a knee; held my sandaled foot. "I meant to do this down at the beach," he began.

I was raised to make a man wait, so as to super-charge my allure. By this point in my life, it was a habit. I smiled into his eyes and said I needed to think about it.

"Very good!" he said, a little too loudly. I could see him clinging to the scene's romantic possibilities; the glass-strewn lot, my roiling stomach could be part of a cute story one day.

That night, we slept together. I was housesitting for a unit publicist I knew. She was constantly being flown around the country to work on location. Her bathroom cabinets overflowed with hotel toiletries. Our sleeping together was chaste. Leon and I both wore the unit publicist's sweatshirts and pants. We fell asleep holding hands like a couple of stuffed otters.

When I awoke, he'd left for work. He must have walked his motorcycle to the corner to avoid waking me. I would have welcomed a roar.

Over backdoor cigarettes, I told my neighbor, Thora, what had happened. In her heyday, Thora had been one of those piano bar chanteuses who peppered her set with world-weary patter. But now she was retired, in the caftan and rattan furniture phase of life.

Thora took my toddler hands in her own. "We'll plan the nuptials together," she rasped. She raised her arms and tossed her hair, her naked body visible through the batwing sleeve opening of her caftan.

How does anyone know when they are in their heyday, in the right location? I hated my job but loved the view. The building was across Santa Monica Boulevard from the Los Angeles Country Club. From the 14th floor, L.A. looked like a verdant plain. Jets ripped soft trails across the sky. Once I shook Magic Johnson's hand in the high-speed elevator.

It was time for work. In the basement, it looked as if no one was on duty. Here was my hope for Leon: that he'd roared off on his motorcycle in furious dismissal of me. Toward a wild future in a big-sky location like Yuma or Kansas City.

But there he was, hunched like a fussbudget, retrieving a scatter of safety pins from the floor. I began to duck below the tall counter. But it was too late.

"I was just . . . peering," I said.

"I always did give in to peer pressure," he said. His half-glasses were a little steamed.

I shook my head; kindly, I hope. He nodded in understanding.

Leon was no showstopper, but he had put a little spring in my step. Part of me wishes I was still there in the basement of that Beverly Hills skyscraper. Curled up on the warm cement floor as above me plastic-wrapped dresses and jackets churned their oval trajectory.

Oh, Leon. I would have fallen for you hard, if only you had left me behind.

OTHER PEOPLE'S MOTHERS

Other people's mothers' hair is the shade of a new penny. When their husbands take a powder, they hire us to paint their bedrooms lavender. We take breaks to lift the lids of shoe boxes stacked in the closet. Ooh and aah over what's inside.

Garish sewing projects are strewn around the house. I don't mean Butterick and Simplicity blouses and capris for daughters to wear. These are community theater people. They sew costumes by hand while show tunes blare. *You're a Good Man, Charlie Brown*, *Man of La Mancha*, and *Jesus Christ Superstar*. They belt out snatches of *Liza with a Z* at home, at Circus Donuts, and at the Del Amo Mall.

Other people's mothers have a ribald gap between their two front teeth. They purchase a hat stand and sprinkle it with glitter. They own and wear a Sherlock Holmes hat and cape.

They are doing *Oliver!* They are doing *The Scottish Play*. They are doing a star turn in *Auntie Mame*.

When they leave for the theater, we make schnapps shakes and climb onto the roof. We pitch an army tent on the bleached front lawn.

Monet's mother refers to herself as an old broad. Back home in Georgia, she was called "Toppy." Her father, an itinerant preacher, believed she favored hats. In fact, Monet told me, it was her male classmates' name for her, after her round and sweatered tits. She learned to read from Burma Shave signs.

Spangled with paint, we set out the candles, the Ouija board and its magic plastic planchette. We take off our clothes and pull on cocktail dresses and costume jewelry of Toppy's. We place beside the Ouija board the kitchen cleaver from the bottom kitchen drawer. The candlelight flickers against the blade, the walls. We sprawl across the fragrant bed, trying to channel Marilyn Monroe.

Toppy keeps her thin nightgown under the pillow. In the morning, we will see her in it, red hair undone. We will see her slender shadowy figure inside. Her face is worn without her makeup.

Toppy is packing for a weekend in Palm Springs with an old man named Jerry, a union rep down at the harbor who can't believe his good fortune. He has taken us to the Magic Castle so we'll like him more. Monet argues with him about the Sears Wish Book, about everything.

Jerry gives up and returns to his wife. Toppy rents an apartment near Fairfax and 3rd, temping for minimum wage and working the Renaissance Faire with members of her coven. She wears her Sherlock Holmes hat and cape to work. She stretches her lipsticked mouth over that wide gap-toothed smile.

When you meet someone else's parent for the first time, they are already whole and finished. You don't have that visceral expertise that you have of your own mother and father, whose smells and habits and little reflexive utterances you fully own.

There is nothing like divorce to shake up the finished whole, open it wide. Spit it out into the sun's harsh light. For the adult to become a human being who sings and slumps and cries and breaks apart in their yearning for love.

Who dies too poor, too young. A month behind on rent. A pair of her false eyelashes like mating spiders on the hospice end table.

STAIN

Tom's Impala pulls onto Alice's street, her house of windows lidded with wooden and peeked-through blinds. In the kitchen, Alice's mother stops her dishwashing motions, then resumes.

"See you." Alice calls out and leaves to meet her supervisor. No . . . her lover. Other than the artist who inked her shoulder back at college, Tom is the only person who has ever seen Alice's tattoo. Old-fashioned tea roses in a bunch. Ironically, her mother would appreciate the design, the detail.

Alice closes the front door behind her and smooths her dress. Outside and in, Tom's car is so white, she squints.

He reaches across the leather expanse to unlatch the passenger door. "Hey." Sexy lines appear at the edges of his smile.

Sexy. Alice thinks in such terms now. It's partly college, but mostly of her knowledge of sexual matters has come after her return to her parents' home.

"Hey." She breathes in the car's smell: leather seats mingled with Tom's citrusy aftershave. The dash lights before them. Sharp. No, impeccable.

After Alice dropped her classes and returned home, her parents said she could either register at the junior college or get a job. She's been pulling down six weekly dinner shifts at Piper's, the local chop house.

Last night, in the parking lot, Tom had breathed into her ear while he was still inside her, "I am your slaaaaave." All day long, making her bed, helping her mother with the shopping, bleaching the tub, and dressing for their date, Alice has pulled this utterance out to savor.

Now she puts her hand on Tom's arm, breathes: "I need to feel you." He actually gulps; she sees it with a little thrill. How sophisticated to have a married lover to excite with commands.

This stage of her life is a transit point, Alice knows. Her old bedroom with its lilac walls, lunch with her parents at the maple kitchen table. Smiling for customers at Piper's and the fumbling experiments in the parking lot. Now sleeping with a married man who lives with his wife, baby, and in-laws in the town of Alice's tap dancing, sewing, straight-A childhood.

Before too many years have passed, these weeks will seem like a mild and slightly unsavory season in which Alice's tip money grew. In which mornings were spent lolling in bed with a book while her mother watered the yard, believing Alice was sleeping in. In which Alice sewed seven dresses to herald her arrival to her future life—her *real* life— like coolly fantastic flags.

After Tom has made love to her, the bottom half of Alice's face pulses with heat. His beard has scraped her. Retrieving her underpants, she sees her lipstick has rolled from her pocket and opened. A lurid cranberry smear mars the white upholstery of her seat where he cannot see it. Alice doesn't mention it, not wanting to spoil things.

Tom kisses her forehead before entering the avenue, the main street, the wide highway. Red and white and yellow light, just starting to burn.

FLYING

I'm sitting on a metal patio chair on the back deck at my in-laws' place in Mexico City. My ass sticks to the metal through my thin dress. My husband's aunt lives on the ground floor. I can hear her singing loudly to the radio: "Big Old Jet Airliner."

I have not exactly come outside to escape my husband and my in-laws. But there is nowhere to comfortably sit in their cramped apartment. The daybed in the living room is high up. I think my mother-in-law, an energetic blonde, sleeps there. And the leather couch is covered in fleece throws because the dogs sleep there. My father-in-law has recently discovered weed, and the whole place smells like the inside of Cheech and Chong's van.

Inside, my husband and his mother are hunched over the computer, scanning ancestry websites. In his room, my father-in-law reclines in front of the fan, wrinkled hands curled around his bong. Adding a hair-raising occasional surprise are the parrots, Tito and Pupi, who are allowed to fly freely around the apartment. I believe Tito and Pupi are the reason for my father-in-law's high blood pressure, although he says it's his exposure to Agent Orange during Vietnam. I have barely slept since our arrival four days ago.

My husband's aunt switches to "Dirty Deeds Done Cheap," but her lusty voice is immediately obscured by the roar of a motorcycle entering the tiny parking lot I'm overlooking.

Another relative? No, it's the Chinese food we have ordered. I hear my husband's aunt saying we are all upstairs, and to my surprise, a skinny old guy in a white t-shirt and black jeans ascends the back stairs to where I am sitting. I'd expected him to come around the front.

"Rosalba Murillo?" he asks, and I nod yes. It really is a shame I have lost all my Spanish. He sets two bulging plastic sacks down on the patio table and after I determine he already has the credit card number, I sign my mother-in-law's name, adding a whopping tip.

Downstairs, Tia Diana is belting out "Smoke on the Water." Inside, Tito and Pupi are shrieking. My father-in-law has switched his television on and laughs boomingly at a variety show he watches every evening at this time.

I curve my hands in front of my chest, puppy style, then rotate them in imitation of a motorcycle throttling. The delivery man laughs, showing a crooked smile with gold at the back. He has turquoise paint spattering the front of his jeans. And I can see he isn't all that old. He extends a hand and I follow him barefoot in my sundress. I hop on the back of the bike. The seat sears my thighs. Before we leave the city limits, my hair is dry.

GOING PUBLIC

"'How 'bout this shit, Ang?" Angela's twin sister was slouched in the loveseat, bare feet splayed atop the coffee table. "Director and screenwriter John Guerrero financed his micro-budget first film by allowing his body to be used for medical experiments."

Angela was curled up in Edgardo's recliner, work shoes cast off on the carpet beside her. She'd released her curly hair from the big barrette that held it during her shifts waiting tables at The Meat Up.

"Sounds like one stand-up cholo," Angela replied. Noticing Edgardo, she said, "Hear that, babe? What that crazy guy did for art?"

"That's dedication," Edgardo returned, keeping it light. The odor of fruit mingled with the ammoniac tang of the hair dye he'd used before dinner. The gloves that came in the package were laughably dainty; Edgardo'd had to use plastic grocery bags. He pierced another peach. The butter crust waited, thumb-pressed into the tin. In the sink, the dinner dishes—with the pastry cutter, mixing bowl attachments, and spoons—soaked in hot, soapy water. He wasn't changing his hair color or anything, just fixing those white strands that threaded the black. He took after his mother. "Anyone want coffee?"

"Extra hot, hon," Cuca cracked.

If Cuca never returned to Boyd and lived with Edgardo and Angela for the remainder of time, Edgardo would never,

ever get used to the sound of his sweet wife's voice defiled into ragged coughing. His bride's mouth screwed around a cigarette.

"No coffee for me," said Angela. I'm still wired from work. Wired and tired."

"My love." Edgardo stepped over, rubbed her cool bare feet.

"They let Edgardo and Shirleen go, and now the rest of us just bust our asses twice as hard."

Cuca butted in. "But that movie *vato* wasn't waiting around waiting for his ship to come in, though."

Angela shrugged. "Gotta hand it to a guy who'll go that extra mile."

"Thank you, Horatio Alger," Edgardo snapped. Was it triumph he read on his sister-in-law's face before it was covered by the hysterical glee of her magazine's cover girl?

Five months had passed since The Meat Up let Edgardo go. It wasn't him, it wasn't his cooking, just that times were tough. People were going out less. This was the San Fernando Valley, not West L.A. or Santa Monica. They'd keep Leroi, who had a kid. They'd keep Angela.

The next morning after dropping Angela off at The Meat Up, Edgardo called the UCLA Medical Center and asked whether they were conducting any paid medical studies. After being advised where he could find the current announcements, he barreled the pickup down Sepulveda to Westwood.

At the Medical Center's bulletin board, he collected paper tabs. He did all this to prove a point: the fact that he wasn't t-shirt cannoning the Valley with resumes had nothing to do with unwillingness to pull his weight.

Edgardo and his sisters had grown up in San Antonio without a man in the house. Their father's lonely hauls back and forth the eye-10 paid the rent and put food on the table and clothes on their backs, but it was at the cost of his absence. The year he turned twelve, Edgardo had surged up like a sunflower, gaining eleven inches in height over one year. His bones would ache at night, his big feet dangling from the edge of his boyhood bed. His mother assured him the pain meant he was growing into a strong man. But Edgardo didn't want to become a giant wretch who belonged to the world and the interstate. He wanted to stay with his mother and help her make fried herring and *kroppkakor*.

He began working after school in his Uncle Hans and Aunt Linda's roadside cafe, filling water glasses and clearing plates. Later, he'd begun slanging hamburgers and patty melts. Edgardo's goal was to have his own business by the time he was thirty.

In the medical center's "Healing Garden," Edgardo settled himself on a scrolled bench and began calling the numbers from the slips he'd collected. He discarded the studies that requested female subjects. Most of the lines patched him straight through to voicemail. One study entailed having your throat numbed and an apparatus inserted to monitor your lungs. "You will experience a significant amount of discomfort," the gal who answered advised him breathlessly. Finally, he was down to his last chance. The white scrap read, "Vitamin E Study." The researcher answered halfway through the first ring.

Compared to the lung thing, this one sounded civilized: the administration of Vitamin E and some other medication, and a few blood draws over a ten-hour period to check the interaction of the two. Since he was already nearby, he agreed to a general pre-screening of urine and blood. He strode to the meeting like a man with a purpose. If this worked out, he'd be doing his bit to advance medical science, contributing to the store of human knowledge. Okay!

The building where Naomi the researcher said to meet her for the pre-screening was a utilitarian stucco affair behind the medical center and through an outdoor freight area. A sheet of paper affixed to the glass entrance read, "Medical Study Area! Room 404." He jogged the three flights, pushed open a swinging door.

Inside the bright-lit room, five or six people, a couple of them attached by rubber tubes to IV stands, lounged in folding chairs around a circular table, watching television or hunched over their phones. A couple of stringy-haired guys in pajamas were comparing stories about Robbie Knievel, son of the famous daredevil. Several hospital beds lined one wall, some partially hidden by screens. The room was like a combination waiting room and a shabby hospital suite.

"Mr. Axelson?" A smiling woman approached, buttoning her white smock.

"Hey." Edgardo shook her outstretched hand, marveling at its daintiness. " Her name tag read, "Naomi Tsukimura, Pharm. D., Research Fellow." He wasn't sure what he was supposed to call her.

"Ready?" she asked brightly, already leading him to a cluttered work desk at the back of the room, crowded with IV stands, tubes, vials, opened boxes of medical supplies, and a menacing-looking red plastic tub marked "for disposal of infectious waste." She didn't introduce him to any of the IV people. A Chicano dude dressed like Naomi sat with them, his nose in a spy novel.

Edgardo cleared his throat. She hadn't said anything about putting on a show. This was his *blood*. "Can I lie down? Could I get a folding screen?" he asked.

"No problem," Naomi returned. She got him settled on one of the cots, had him roll up his sleeve, and tightened a yellowish strip of rubber around his arm. He closed his eyes, heard the sound of a packet being torn. The sharp scent of rubbing alcohol. She swiped roughly at the inside of his arm.

"I'm good," he said for the benefit of the others in the room. He felt certain they had their ears pricked after he'd requested privacy.

He hadn't had his blood drawn since he and Angela applied for their marriage license. The wedding at L.A. City Hall seemed long ago, although less than a year had passed. Shirleen and LeRoi had been their witnesses, and they'd all gone to the Biltmore for drinks after, none of them with a notion of knowing the events awaiting the newlyweds: Edgardo's layoff, the impossibility of finding work. Cuca's noisy arrival. Angela's sadness.

"Who submits to these tests, anyway?" he asked, wanting to place himself outside the population of this strange world of hospital food, of medicines and blood vials.

"Oh, sometimes residents and interns," she answered, still swiping. "They can use the money, plus they happen to be in the neighborhood. I used myself as a subject for this one." She laughed and stuck him.

Edgardo counted ceiling tiles until Naomi withdrew the needle and pressed a square of cotton to the inside of his elbow. He heard a tube being capped. She said Edgardo could rest if he wanted. He did feel a little woozy. She set a plastic cup on the bed beside his shoulder, saying the bathroom was just on the other side of the swinging door, when he was ready. A moment later, Edgardo rose, setting his feet gingerly on the floor. He pushed back the folding screen, cutting an embarrassed glance to the television area.

He crossed the room, arms folded to hide the cup. He hoped he had enough for the test. The Chicano guy glanced at him; away.

On his way back with the filled cup, Edgardo didn't bother trying to hide its contents. This was a place of medicine. Blood and pee and worse were no big deal here. Organs and pus were their bread and butter! Naomi sat at the technician's desk, on which sat a rack of filled and labeled blood vials. He set the cup of urine beside it.

Naomi gave him some paperwork to read at home. Beginning at noon the next day, Edgardo would spend ten hours here. Nice. He'd pictured himself alone in a pleasant, secluded room, reading magazines.

"Well, I have to get these into the refrigerator now," Naomi said. She offered Edgardo her hand, finished with him until the next day.

The screening hadn't been painful, and Naomi seemed to know what she was doing. But the thought of her inserting a catheter (Like a little faucet! she'd supplied cheerfully), pulling blood from his body eleven separate times during the next day made Edgardo twist and fidget all night. It was nearly six by the time he finally slipped into sleep. Angela woke him at ten, as he'd requested, shaking him gently by the shoulder. Leroi would pick her up for work in a minute.

The blood draw spot at the inside of Edgardo's right elbow was stained purple. Any effect his dramatic gesture might have provided had already been made. Now the idea seemed ludicrous: that a man might need literal blood money to make points with his own wife. Still curled in their bed. Edgardo read aloud from one of the forms Naomi had given him: "Participation in this study is strictly voluntary. As an experimental subject I have the right to refuse to participate at all or to change my mind about participation after the study is started if I have reservations." Angela, combing her wet hair, smiled encouragingly.

"If I wish to participate, I should sign below."

"Sounds legit." Angela dipped to tie her work shoes; the back of her white blouse was wetted translucent by her hair in a seaweed-like pattern. She was working a double today.

"What if I have reservations, Angela. It's—macabre!" Edgardo grimaced, wanting her to agree, wanting the backing out, his distaste for the medical study, to belong to both of them. Something they'd smile about someday when Cuca was gone.

But Angela's expression was neutral. They stared at one another in their newly familiar roles: Edgardo the fuck-up, Angela disappointed once again.

"Baby, it's been so tough," she said. "This isn't . . . what I thought marriage would be like." She eyed him as though to measure how large an explosion her comment might spark. Did she think he was going to yell or throw a chair with Cuca right there in the kitchen, frying up breakfast sausages?

Edgardo rose. Began yanking the sheets from their bed, flinging them into the corner hamper. He grabbed at the shopping bag on his side, withdrew the packaged white bedding he'd picked up at Pier One on the way home from UCLA. He used his teeth to tear the plastic wrapping, then opened the folded top sheet, tried to shake it out between them.

"Let me help." Angela took one edge of the sheet, tried to pull it away. But the sheet, still folded so tightly from the package, wouldn't pull away.

"Forget it!" Then, with more kindness than he felt: "It's late."

He wanted her out of the house so he could hear himself think. As though Edgardo were a sick child, she kissed his brow, patted his hand, then left the room, half-shutting the door behind her.

In the kitchen, the landline rang. "Hey, if that's Boyd, tell him I'm not here. Tell him I'm with my new squeeze—a cop!" Idiot.

He located the fitted sheet, bonneted the elastic ends around each corner of the mattress, jaw hardening at the festive buzz of the coffee grinder. He'd stay right where he was until they were on their merry ways: Angela to The Meat Up, Cuca out looking at apartments.

Lou Reed, Angela's stocky white shorthair, emerged from under the bed. The cat had the depthless expression of a bully. In their early days, Lou Reed would practically claw the hollow-core bedroom door from its frame while Edgardo and Angela were making love. Finally, they'd started letting Lou stay, perched like a child king on the red velvet bedside chair, watching.

Edgardo tolerated the cat reluctantly, although he'd long ago stopped bringing Lou dried fish treats and rubber toys in the hope of winning him over. The only diversion the little bastard enjoyed was a cat o' nine tails Angela'd found on the sidewalk in front of the apartment building back when Lou was a kitten. She could send the cat into paroxysms of feline glee by shaking the whip.

When Angela was around, Edgar made a point of acting friendly to Lou, even patting a fat haunch or scratching behind an ear, but alone with the fat feline, Edgardo's policy was to ignore him.

Lou jumped to the mattress, insinuated himself onto Edgardo's lap. "Move your ass," Edgardo muttered. He lifted Lou's bulk and dumped him to the floor.

So this wasn't what Angela thought marriage would be like. He grabbed her pillow, inhaling her scent. His wife. He wrapped himself around the pliant substitute. As if Edgardo himself had envisioned this dissolve into the housecleaning and the cleaning of the litter box, the grocery shopping, the budget movie matinees.

He leapt from the bed, slapped the shade spinning on its upper rod. He pulled on a pair of sweats and moved to the kitchen, which was dirty but deserted. The air was thick with the smell of sausage and burnt coffee and Cuca's morning cigarette. The stove top was gooey with butter and cold meat grease.

A folded piece of notebook paper lay on the kitchen table, his name written in pencil. Angela had left a note. *"I shouldn't have said what I did."* She didn't say she was sorry. She didn't take it back. He'd been the good little houseboy for the past five months, hadn't he, serving up dinners, cleaning up the messes? Tolerating Cuca's derisive cackle, her comments about how well Angela was taking it?

Did Angela imagine this was what Edgardo thought his life would be like at twenty-nine, that he'd look ahead of him and have not a clue in the colorless sky what his next step should be? That humorless children in suits and expensive shoes, barely off the playground, would be asking in disbelief why he wasn't Microsoft Office proficient.

That's when Edgardo sprang into action. Pulse dancing, he crammed jeans, shirts, and underwear into the new pillowcases. Outside, he threw open the Scion's door and dumped the whole mess into the back seat. He'd dress, leave food and water for Lou Reed, and get the hell out.

He shook the last of Lou's dry food into the cat bowl. The cat: where was that prick? Edgardo checked under the bed, his own side of the closet, a tumble of worn black shoes. Next, under the stove, behind the icebox, amidst the dirty clothes smelling faintly of mildew in the bathroom hamper: favorite Lou hangouts. Damn it: the front door was hanging open.

The guest room was next. Cuca'd left an explosion of blouses and pants slung wildly over chairs. Capless spray bottles filled the room with intoxicating, unknown aromas, the smells of a stranger. Cuca said she didn't mind if he worked at his desk while she was out, but he hadn't entered since her arrival.

"Lou?" He bent, shook Cuca's blankets, inhaled her scent, tart and springy. Her smoky, female shit spread around in here made him jittery.

"Hey, Prince Charming!" Cuca cried, standing in the doorway. Her mouth was stained with heavy, berry-colored lipstick. She leered mock-appreciatively at Edgardo's hairless chest.

"Hey," Edgardo managed, moving past her into the kitchen. "Seen Lou?"

"All I ever see of that beast is an asshole and a tail. He hates me," she returned, dumping the contents of the ashtray in the trash and lighting another cigarette.

"Maybe he dislikes secondhand smoke," Edgardo sniffed.

"OK, OK. Sorry about the mess. Don't clean, dude. I'm serious; I'll get it after my interview." He watched her walk away, her round ass the spitting image of Angela's.

He was still holding the cat o' nine tails. "Lou?" His voice was rusty. Edgardo rattled the soft leather fringes of the whip, murmuring extravagant curses and the cat's name—worthless, whoever heard of a cat that came when you called it?

He slapped the chairback with the whip. He'd do it, go through with the stupid medical study. He'd need the money out there on his own, anyway. He hit the chair again, harder this time.

"Find what you're looking for?" Cuca. Now with just a bra on top. "I gotta change my shirt. Sweaty."

Edgardo moved first, but it wasn't like Cuca pushed him away. In fact, she grabbed him by the head and planted one on his mouth. Deep. A kind of kiss he and Angela hadn't shared in months. And no, it wasn't anything like kissing his wife. There was the cigarette-y taste, of course. He liked it. There were also the sounds she made. A throaty moan. Edgardo was instantly hard.

He had to know.

He lifted Cuca to the desk and pushed her skirt up above her thighs. It was she who pulled the flimsy panty aside, not stopping to take it off. He dove. Tasted. Her intimate cry was loud, louder than Angela ever permitted herself. But the taste. Yes. It was the same.

When it was over, she leaned in and wiped his mouth. Her eyes flicked to his crotch. A dare danced in her expression—so like Angela's in friendlier times.

He squeezed her shoulder.

She caught his hand in hers, gave him a stare.

"I'd better get to that appointment," he managed.

"Good call," she said. "Get outta here."

To save money, he parked at the Federal Building and speed-walked across Wilshire and up to the campus. He jogged through the long corridor of the Medical Center, out the back door, and into the loading area. He sprinted the steps to the study building.

There was no sign of Naomi. In the deserted hall outside the door to the study area, Edgardo removed his watch cap and stuffed it partway into his waistband, then chewed his cuticles, and finally drew the folded release from his pocket.

He said, "On the study day, I will enter the Infusion Therapy and Research Center at 12:00 p.m. at which time a catheter (a small tube that will allow for blood samples to be drawn) will be inserted into a vein in my arm."

The image of the terrible blood faucet came again, and he swallowed back a rush of nausea. C'mon, man. It was only a little blood! Plenty of people gave donations of twice as much as the whole study would take.

"After the insertion of the catheter has been inserted, I will receive a single oral dose of cyclosporine of 10 mg/kg with or without a dose of Liqui-E depending on my randomization. I will then have 2 teaspoons of blood drawn at 0, 0.5, 1, 2, 3, 4, 6, and 8 hours after the cyclosporine dose."

Maybe Naomi was waiting inside the actual study area. He pushed open the swinging door and peered inside.

"May I help you?" At the nearest cot, a kneeling technician, pudgy and blonde, squinted up at him as she fiddled with the stubborn wheel of an elderly Black lady's IV stand.

"I'm meeting one of the researchers—Naomi? I'm a little early."

"Hmm. They run all kinds of studies in here. Make yourself at home." As Edgardo sat at a card table to wait, for Naomi, the subjects of the IV study stood in turn to submit to their technician at her desk: everyone politely ignoring their fellows as blood was drawn, drips attached. Edgardo recognized some of the faces from the previous day. No one looked at him. Puzzlers, acrostics, bead stringing supplies had been left out on a big round dining table. After being connected to one of the rolling IV poles hung with a plastic sack of liquid, a man, pockmarked and skinny, stretched out on the couch and dozed off, face to the ceiling. Something about the setting made Edgardo—no, not feel sick, but feel as though he *were* sick, on the precipice of surrender to a vague and painless torpor, released from time.

The TV was going at low volume: a tell-all talk show. An adopted, middle-aged woman was meeting her mother for the first time. Another case was an engaged couple, the man openly indulging in an affair, which he planned to end on the eve of the wedding. The mistress was there too, in neutral colors, flat shoes, and no makeup, a startling contrast to the fiancée herself. Around the TV, in various positions of repose, the other medical subjects offered suggestions to the fiancée: "Get your GED and take care of number one—that's what I'm doing," a dingy-haired girl in a robe and slippers advised.

"You've got to love yourself first, honey," the pockmarked man sighed without opening his eyes.

A middle-aged lady hmmphed, "Get on with the marriage, and tell that tramp to step off!"

Perhaps as Naomi told him, internists and residents often volunteered. But most of the volunteers, Edgardo realized, were desperate for money. One thing he could say for himself: he'd never sink low enough to follow the soaps or talk shows. Daytime television was for losers.

The overhead lights buzzed. Where was Naomi? Edgardo spotted a water cooler next to the door, and he headed for it. Wrapped in a hospital blanket, somebody slept curled in a gurney. Beside some of the other beds, personal effects were arranged: cheap shampoos and lotions, gossip magazines, several shabby purses. Everything so public.

Nobody said anything to Edgardo, although an addled-looking guy with pumpkin-colored hair and bad teeth nodded and grinned from his seat near the TV.

"Hey, I'm running down the hall for a sec, OK?" the chubby technician announced, and there was a general murmur of agreement from the subjects, Edgardo included.

It was 12:05. Edgardo gathered up the papers, crumbled them, carried the trash to the plastic can at the technician's desk.

Beside the plastic infectious waste jar, a little white stuffed bear holding a puffy red heart had tipped onto its side. "Something to remember me by," a floral enclosure card underneath the bear read.

He squeezed the stuffed bear, which made no sound. The Justice of the Peace Office at L.A. City Hall, where Edgardo and Angela were married, had been festooned with stuffed bears and kittens, handmade cards and streamers, as though the celebrants needed to personalize the occasion, make it memorable to the State clerk who performed the same ceremony hundreds of times a month. As though having an interested and involved witness to the intimate moments of their lives granted courage and validity, made it more probable that you'd honor your own promises.

"Aw," somebody said. The man on TV was crying, saying he couldn't help his ways; he was from a military background. His fiancée opened her arms. The mistress looked as though she didn't know whether she was supposed to leave. It was the mistress, going home by herself, that Edgardo felt for. What would happen to her now?

Edgardo watched the mistress's displacement with horror, half-expecting the television audience to begin shouting, or even throwing items to force her from the stage.

The men's room, he remembered, was just outside the study area door. He headed there under the silent pretext of needing to piss. He didn't want to be shut out in the cold, with no one to care whether he got out of bed in the morning, no one to recognize or scold or remember who he was. Decisively, Edgardo drew the consent form from his back pocket. He wasn't a desperate person. He uncapped his pen extravagantly with his teeth, and printed on the back of the unsigned release, "I am sorry to say I will be unable to participate in the Vitamin E study. Sincerely, Mr. Axelson.

Back in the hall, Edgardo noticed what he hadn't seen before: Naomi had left him a note. He should meet her, not in the testing area, or her office, but the next building over, in room 105. He used the strip of adhesive tape to replace the Naomi's note with his own, fled up the stairs, through the hospital's interminable corridors, past the hospital gift shop, through Westwood Village and across traffic-clogged Wilshire to the parking lot and the Scion.

The tiny lot behind The Meat Up had a space open. Before going inside, Edgardo dragged the suitcase across the wide leatherette seat and yanked it out the driver's side door. The truck bed was crowded with the artifacts of his and Angela's life: the hibachi spilling powdery gray ash. The empty plastic water jugs he kept meaning to fill up at the machine in front of Lucky's. A box of frayed towels. A pink cowboy hat of Angela's. He packed his suitcase down.

As he pulled open the restaurant's heavy glass door, Edgardo was weakened by a sudden loss of nerve: What if, in this public place, Angela were to turn him away? The thought turned his muscles to rubber. He headed straight to table two, in back. No Angela. An old guy sat alone at number four, nursing a full glass of ice water and reading a paperback. At number seven, a big party of suits was drinking and yukking it up. One of the men whispered something to a female colleague, who teasingly poked the man with a finger. And there was Angela, emerging from the little cubicle that connected the restaurant to the bar. She was balancing a round tray of drinks, some of which had umbrellas and fruit-stuck swizzles sticking up from them. Her thick hair spilled from the loose bun at the top of her head. Edgardo was close enough to see the beauty mark at the corner of her mouth.

He watched her work. After distributing the drinks, Angela asked the man at the head of the table if they were ready now. When the man nodded, she set the tray on the floor, leaned it against her leg, and took out her order book. A man in a pastel tie said something and she laughed, showing her dimples.

He waited until her back was to him. Busy taking orders, Angela didn't notice Edgardo pass and enter the empty kitchen. Where was Leroi, the cook? Edgardo lifted the lid of the row of salad canisters, popped a crouton into his mouth. The swinging doors to the dining room parted. Edgardo's wife appeared before him like some kind of prize. "Hey." She seemed pleased but not surprised to see him.

Angela slid the tray under the salad prep counter, drew the ticket pad from her pocket and wrote some more on the top page. "Huge party of shrinks on seven. They're sure making *me* nuts."

"Probably how they get new customers." Edgardo bent to wrap his arms around her He felt like a lover in a movie, meeting his mistress. Leroi lumbered from the back of the kitchen to his station at the grill, holding uncooked pork chops. He scowled under his stiff white hat.

Angela raised a finger to the burly cook. "Hold off on that ticket. A minute with my husband." Leroi said nothing, just tossed the chops from one hand to the other.

Tenderly, Edgardo kissed her upper left arm, and began: "I went for the study."

"You did?" She glanced toward the grill, but Leroi had disappeared. Edgardo was nearly disappointed. He wanted to go public with his devotion, wanted everybody in the goddamned place to know how much he revered her. Hot dishwasher steam issued from around the corner.

"Was it okay? Was it awful?" Angela searched his face. He shrugged, dismissing her concern.

"They canceled. I'm the wrong blood type or something. Angela, it's Lou. He got away, honey." He flashed a quick, lateral palm. "Cuca left the door open." He felt like a doctor breaking unsettling news. "I'm handling everything, baby."

Stricken, she reached for Edgardo's hand. "I know she's my sister, but I've never met anyone more self-absorbed."

The glow came. "Ange, don't be hard on her. I'll make posters, check Animal Control every day," Edgardo said. "Feel like venison chili tonight? She like hot food like we do?"

"Sure, OK. I just can't believe this. I know she's not used to pets, but I *told* her."

"Well, it's a sensitive time. She hides it by cracking jokes and being loud, you know? Let's not tell her it's her fault." He'd pick up some beer, too. He'd freeze it so cold the bottlenecks would be lined with slivers of ice. He'd stop by Ralph's, pick up a slab of venison and the peppers—*anchos*, pickled jalapeños and the small-but-mighty *chilipiquins*. Garlic and cumin seeds, they already had. He'd roast the seeds in the cast-iron skillet, sauté the garlic in Cuca's sausage drippings to give the chili a salty, juicy kick. He'd fix it so hot they'd sweat.

Overcome, Edgardo took his wife's hands in his and sank to his knees. Her fingers smelled of cilantro and vinaigrette.

"Honey?" she said. "What would I do without you?"

If only he could ask her to marry him all over again. They'd face this thing together: locating stubby, bilious Lou, helping Cuca to start her new life. Edgardo and Angela, side by side, would build upon the day-to-day push and pull of vulnerability and strength, building the marriage anew. He could console her all day long.

"C'mon man," Leroi sighed from his station at the grill. On his knees, Edgardo tightened his arms around his wife's thighs, thanking fate for her fingers in his hair, for Leroi as witness to this oh-so-narrow triumph. Edgardo sighed into the flesh of his angel, like a man who had gambled with and been found by the narrowest fraction the victor of a complex and drawn-out malady.

ACKNOWLEDGMENTS

"Company" was published by *Atticus Review*

"Orange, Yellow, and Black OR Everything is Archie" was published in *Pidgeonholes*

"Gone Baby Gone" was published in *X-R-A-Y Lit*

"Hot Dogs" was published in *Wigleaf*

"Over There" was published in *SmokeLong Quarterly* and in *Flash Fiction America* (W.W. Norton)

"Little Will" was published in *Ghost Parachute*

". . . and Title it, Faith" was published in *Reckon Review*

"Anthropology" was published in *Pithead Chapel*

"Three Ways: A Triptych of Love and Its Imprint," "It is the Summer of Skylab," and "Ties That Bind" were published in *FRiGG*

"The Angle of Depression" was published in *Okay Donkey*

"Before the Election" was published in *Milk Candy Review*

"Codpod" was published in *Ghost Parachute*

"Flux" was published in *Newfound, An Inquiry of Place*, and in *Best Small Fictions 2023* (Electric Lit)

"Lucky Day" was published by Reflex Press and in *Blue Bob, an Anthology* (Cowboy Jamboree Press)

"The Gap Year" was published in *Little Patuxent Review*

"I Mean, Norman!" was published in *The Phare*

"17 Reasons Why" was published in *Bending Genres*

"I'm In You" was published in *trampset*

"The New Span" was published in *Twin Pies Lit*

"Pardon Me for Moonwalking" was published in *No Contact Magazine*

"Closing Time" was published in *100 Word Story*

"Man on the Moon" was published in *Flash Frog*

"Loosies" was published in *Litro Magazine*

"We Are All Sitting Down to Miracle Monday" was published in *The Pinch*

"Buckets" was published in *Citron Review*

"Everything is About to Go Wrong, But So Far It Hasn't" was published in *Crack the Spine*

"Oxygen" was published in *Ellipsis Zine*

"Your Home Town" was published in *In Defense of Pseudoscience* (Reflex Press)

"The Little Jenny" was published in *Invisible City*

"Husbandry" was published in *Barren Magazine*

"The Ghost of Charles Bukowski Pines for His Job at the Mails" was published in *Flash Frog*

"The Altogether" was published in *Riggwelter*

"Trust" was published in *Ellipsis Literature and Art*

"Rat Girl" was published in *Sou'wester* (print) and *Fractured Lit* (online)

"Country Music" was published in *Tiny Molecules*

"The Other Susana" was published by *805 Lit+Art*

"Not Nowadays, and Never Here" was published in *Jarnal* (Mason Jar Press)

"So You Think You Can Tell" was published in *Pithead Chapel*

"Antwerp Zoo Says Woman Who Had 'Affair' with Chimp Must Stay Away for 'His Health'" was published in *Twin Pies Lit*

"In the Midst of a Global Pandemic, Your Washing Machine Gives Up the Ghost" was published in *Flash Flood Journal*

"Chalk Outline" was published in *BULL*

"In The Back Yard" was published in *Bracken Journal*

"To the Woman Pacing in Circles in Front of the Elementary School, Her Fresh-Groomed Dog Trotting Alongside" was published in *South Florida Poetry Journal*
"Location" was published in *New Flash Fiction Review*
"Other People's Mothers" was published in *New Flash Fiction Review*
"Stain" was published in *New Flash Fiction Review*
"Flying" was published in *Blue Fifth Review*
"Going Public" was published in *Cowboy Jamboree*

I am grateful to the editors of these journals, and to Meg Pokrass, Nancy Stohlman, Sarah Freligh, and Kathy Fish for your teaching and the inspiration I've found in your works and lives; and Trinidad Bidar, Melody Seguine, Susan Deming, Tom Luttrell, the Flash Monsters!! and the Flash Avengers for their encouragement and verve.

To the late Susie Fought, I'd have changed the world for you if I could have. Thank you for 20 years of being the most enthusiastic reader I could ever ask for. I'll miss your written responses that so often began with, "Fucking hell, Patricia!"

ABOUT PATRICIA Q. BIDAR

Patricia Quintana Bidar is a Los Angeles native whose first publication came at age 58. Her short works have appeared in Waxwing, Wigleaf, Smokelong Quarterly, The Pinch, Atticus Review, and Moon City and have been widely anthologized including in Flash Fiction America (W.W. Norton), Best Small Fictions 2023 and 2024 (Alternating Current), and Best Microfiction 2023 (Pelekinesis Press). Patricia's novelette, Wild Plums (ELJ Press) is available from Amazon. She lives with her family and unusual dog outside of Oakland, California. Visit patriciaqbidar.com

ABOUT THE PRESS

Unsolicited Press is based out of Portland, Oregon and focuses on the works of the unsung and underrepresented. As a womxn-owned, all-volunteer small publisher that doesn't worry about profits as much as championing exceptional literature, we have the privilege of partnering with authors skirting the fringes of the lit world. We've worked with emerging and award-winning authors such as Amy Shimshon-Santo, Brook Bhagat, Elisa Carlsen, Tara Stillions Whitehead, and Anne Leigh Parrish.

Learn more at unsolicitedpress.com. Find us on Instagram, X, Facebook, Pinterest, Bsky, Threads, YouTube, and LinkedIn. Unsolicited Press also writes a snarky newsletter on Substack.